DEMONIC ANTHOLOGY VOLUME V
A Dark Humor Short Story Collection

DEMONIC VACATIONS
Go Home Already!

DEMONIC ANTHOLOGY VOLUME V
A Dark Humor Short Story Collection

DEMONIC
VACATIONS
Go Home Already!

Includes Stories By:

Al Hagan	Alexander C. Bailey	DJ Tyrer	Erika Lance
Evan Baughfman	Georgia Cook	Joseph Valadez
Laura G. Kaschak	Mark Robinson	Mark Towse
Rebecca Rowland	Valerie Willis	W.T. Paterson

4 Horsemen
Publications, Inc.

4 Horsemen
Publications, Inc.

4 Horsemen Publications, Inc.
1497 Main St. Suite 169
Dunedin, FL 34698
4horsemenpublications.com
info@4horsemenpublications.com

Cover by Valerie Willis
Typesetting by Autumn Skye
Editor JM Paquette

Library of Congress Control Number: 2021948214

Print: 978-1-64450-287-7
Ebook: 978-1-64450-288-4

TABLE OF CONTENTS

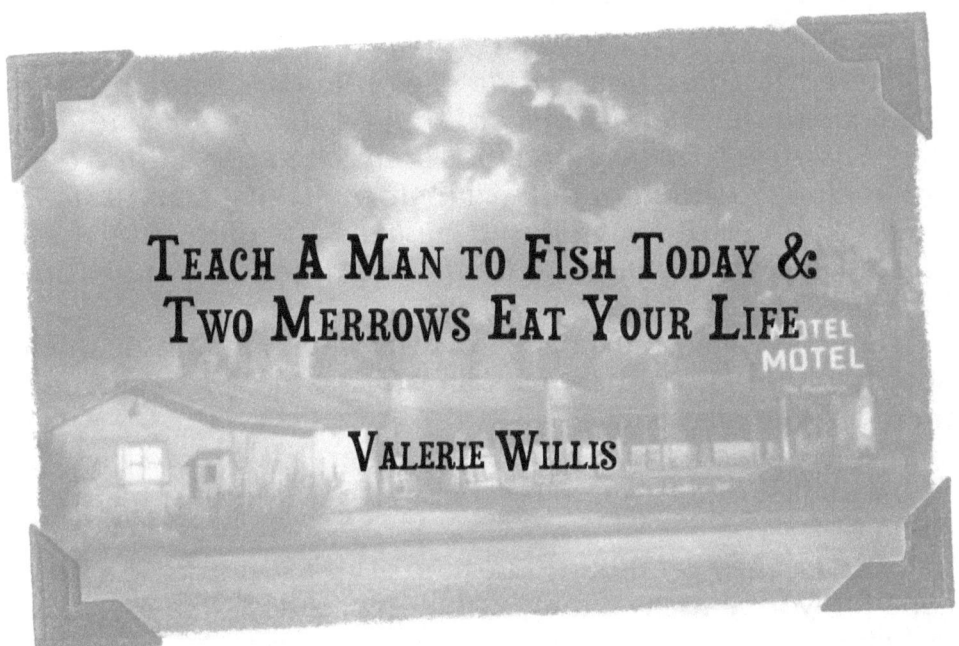

Teach a Man to Fish Today & Two Merrows Eat Your Life

Valerie Willis

Arms wide, embracing the salty breeze, I stood on Ireland's coastline. *I'm here!* It had been my dream since Granny revealed we had Irish blood to visit here. Seagulls squawked as if to blare, *tourist!* Folding my arms, I ended the embrace and turned back to the restaurant. I sat back down in my seat in front of *Keating's Bar and Restaurant*. My husband lifted an eyebrow while he enjoyed his *Kilbaha Bay Crab Claws*. I had ordered a bowl of chowder, watching the steam float off on the breeze like today's plans.

"Sorry. I couldn't help myself." Sighing, I sipped my latte. "You think the captain will change his mind about cancelling today's fishing excursion?"

"I doubt it, babe." He speared a chunk of crab meat with his fork, dunking it into the white sauce. Chewing his food, he managed to say, "It's choppy out there."

Jacob's right.

The tops of the waves were jagged and white, the shallow depths enough to make the water rougher. The water crashed against a rocky shore, white curtains shooting upward and the wind sweeping it away. Despite our seat near the water's edge, sea water never sprayed our table.

1

There's nothing like Florida's shorelines of endless sand. I've been in thunderstorms, lightning striking all around us. Hell, I was on a twenty-one-foot boat when the engine died, and we were walled in with two-story swells. Dad thought we'd have to call for help, but he fixed the engine. A wave had choked the exhaust, killing the oxygen to the pistons.

"Anne."

"Huh?" I broke my grimace from the water, and my husband shook his head. "Honey, we can ask again or maybe see if there's some alternative."

"S-sure." Spooning up some chowder, I accepted my fate. "It just sucks. He offered to reschedule for tomorrow, but we're flying out."

"At least they refunded our deposit. Back home, if a hurricane hit, you're lucky if they're that generous." He shoved the last clump of crab meat. "Man, this will ruin me. *Red Lobster's* snow crab legs won't cut it anymore."

I smiled. "I haven't had a chowder like this since I was a kid. I'm glad we found this place."

"Ma'am?" I turned around, an Irish accent calling my attention. "Did I hear you wanted to go fishing?"

Leaning back into my seat, I locked gazes with an elderly woman sipping her coffee, her long white hair tossing into the wind. Her appearance was how I imagined the Irish Pirate Queen Grace O'Malley to look the night she terrorized the Spanish off Florida's coast: a white night gown, sword raised, and lightning striking at her back!

"That's right. We were supposed to go with the *Fishing Adventures* place up the road here, but the weather is supposed to only get worse."

"Ah, I see." She folded her paper and pondered, "Did you try the other side of County Clare?"

"Sorry, I'm as touristy as it gets. I can't seem to wrap my head on where the county areas are." I blushed. "But, I assume if this is like Florida, it's on the other side of the peninsula?"

"You're a bright one." She chuckled, winking at me. "It's alright, lass. But yes, you can fish off the Kilkee pier. It's only about a thirty-minute drive northeast. Right down R487, the road right here, in fact."

I looked to my husband who folded his brow in thought. "That might work. If it's like back home, the pier might provide tourist packages, and there's a chance the water is deeper on that side."

"Oh, it's deeper alright." The old woman took another sip of her coffee, a glitter in her eye. "My husband and I live on that side, but I grew up here in the bay and come back from time to time to enjoy its waters."

"Thank you." I smiled, turning back to my chowder. "Looks like I might get my Irish fishing trip after all." I lowered my voice. "Should we buy her coffee as a thank you?"

The husband leaned over and shook his head. "Too late. She's gone."

Startled, I twisted back, the table empty save an empty coffee cup and pages of a newspaper fluttering in the wind.

How on earth did she vanish so fast?

The old woman had steered us in the right direction. As promised, half an hour later, we were standing on a sand and rock shoreline filled with boats and fellow fishermen. Now, who would be willing to take us fishing? Walking down the docks, I paused to stare aimlessly at the ocean. No white caps snarled at me here, but the waters were darker, deeper. With an inhale, I took in the salty scent as if enjoying the subtle differences in the smells of roses.

So different than the waters back home. Florida just feels wild and bright with life. Here, in Ireland, there's this ancient and aged beauty to it all. Deep green and earth-toned rock cliffs look like the gods of old dropped them here like a child's building blocks.

"Who're you looking for?" Shaking my head, I realized my husband had left me behind and an old sailor in brown waders gnawed on his pipe staring at me. "Not too many tourists give a glad eye to the ocean. You lose a loved one to the sea?"

"Ah, n-no." Mustering a smile, I revealed my secret. "Since I was small, I've always loved going fishing and everything to do with the ocean. Always reading books and pissing off my high school Marine Biology teacher over how much I knew."

He laughed, nodding. "You plan on fishing today?"

My smile broke. "I *had* plans. The fishing excursion we had planned cancelled since the bay was too rough. They offered to reschedule, but we're heading back to the states tomorrow."

"What a shame. Real shame that is." He gnawed on his pipe, combing his fingers through his beard.

"There you are." My husband had circled back. "You can't just stop like that without telling me."

The sailor narrowed his eyes and a smile broke out. "I'll take you fishing."

"Ah, that would be so cool." I lit up. *How cool to fish with a local instead! This is more our speed!*

"Oh man, I'd love that, but we don't have a temporary license." Jacob rubbed his neck, his mind in super thinking mode. "We were aiming to go with a charter for that reason or maybe see if there was some package for pier access here."

"I haven't done a charter in a while, but my license is good." The old man was shuffling in his many pockets and produced a paper. "Here we go." Unfolding it, he showed us his proof of his Charter and license expiration. "Still good, ya see."

"Well," I looked to my husband with puppy dog eyes, "I'm willing to go. Are you?"

"Psh!" Jacob gave me a skeptical look. "I rather fish with a local than the charter."

"We've got a deal then?" A plume of smoke boiled from his smile.

"Uh, well I suppose first we should discuss the price?" I pulled in my excitement. "We were going to pay €450 for a full day, but how about €300 for about two or so hours?"

The old fisherman held out a hand. "That seems fair. Curious to see how you do out there."

We followed him to the old boat and nostalgia filled me. It was about the size of my Dad's last boat before divorce wrecked all that I held dear. Climbing on board, he tossed us some weather worn life vests and we were off. Feeling the rocking of the hull on the rolling waves and the familiar slap of water brought a sense of freedom. The grin on my face made my cheeks ache, and every time I glanced at Jacob, he chuckled at me.

Fishing trip is happening! YES!

The motor slowed, and the old man came away from the wheelhouse and started to drop anchor. My husband and I lurched forward to offer a hand of help, and he waved us away. Pulling a lever, the anchor slammed into the deep blue waters with a loud splash. The chain hissed and rumbled for quite a while before stopping and going slack. He tilted his hat to us, a smile wide on his face.

"Don't hesitate to put me to work." Jacob was beside himself and eager to start fishing. "I ain't afraid to bait a hook, sir."

"Captain," corrected the old man. "Captain Coomara."

"Captain Coomara." I smiled. "I can bait my own hook as well. Just let me know what I need to do since I've never fished here before."

"Ah, you're fine." The old man rummaged through a panel in the floor and pulled out two heavy and thick rods. "You two okay with bottom fishing?"

"Yes, sir—Captain." Jacob's face reddened, catching himself. "We've done it plenty in the intracoastal and ocean back home."

"Good, good." He was checking the weights and line, testing the drag and making adjustments. "I'll bait the hooks. Can't have my guests getting their hands dirty. Ah, there we go. Ladies first."

He handed me the pole, and I was relieved I was familiar with the tackle being used. "Just drop it straight down 'til it hits bottom, right?"

"Yes, ma'am." The sparkle in his eye was teamed with a raise of an eyebrow. "You've definitely done some fishing, gal."

"Heck, she out-fishes me most days." Jacob took the pole from Captain Coomara. "Thank you kindly, Captain."

"Aye, don't thank me until you catch something though." The old man leaned over the edge of the water. "It can be choppy up here, but down there, she's calm as a summer's breeze."

Smiling, I turned to my side of the boat. Flipping the lever on the reel, the line flowed freely, chasing the weight beyond my view and far into the depths below. My finger caressed the line rushing over it. A *thump* vibrated across it, and I closed the lever, setting the drag into active mode.

Daddy always taught me to let it hit bottom, then reel it in about two or three turns.

I did exactly what Dad had taught me time and time again. The weight could be felt scraping rocks or even the sandy bottom. Amazing how much can be translated through the line and rod. The boat tilted one way, then the other. Swells were large, and after being anchored, it made their height far more intimidating. My balance faltered for a split second, my hip jamming into the railing.

Crap, I almost went over!

Unlike the recreational boats I had fished on, this was designed for commercial fishing. The railing was set lower to make it easier for tugging nets on and off the deck. Shuddering, I spaced my feet to gain extra agility and balance. With rough seas, it became a physical endurance game to stay up right. My finger tugged on the line; still no sign of fish. A large swell was rolling in from Jacob's side, under the hull, breaching on my side, and the deck tilted hard. I stumbled few steps back, gripping the railing to keep from falling back—

KASPLASH!

The world slowed, nausea waving over me. Turning, I could see Captain Coomara looking over the railing.

"JACOB!" Dropping my rod, I rushed to his side only to be met with blue water. "JACOB!"

Scrambling, I was tugging on a rope fastened at the wheelhouse. My chest ached, my heart slamming against my sternum. A wave rolled in, the boat tilting again.

He had a life vest! Where did he go? Why isn't he responding!

Looking at the incoming blue swell, orange caught my eye. I tugged harder on the rope, freeing it at last. My eyes found the bright orange, and my body began to shake. Jacob was missing.

6

No way. No way this is happening...

"JACOB! JACOB!" I shrieked, tears falling.

We've been boating and fishing so much, there's no way he would have taken it off.

Closing my eyes, I shook my head.

I need to focus; this isn't the time to break down, Anne!

Opening my eyes, I realized Captain Coomara had gripped my life vest to steady me.

"What are you...?" I paled.

A knife cut the straps of my life vest, and it began to slip off. He gave me a violent shove, my hip catching, and I found myself falling. His shark-tooth grin and pitch-black eyes were the last thing I saw as I sunk into the icy water. The shock of the cold water sent a hard and stiff shiver through my muscles. I managed to hold my breath, but I was sinking as fast as the weights on my line. Eyes stinging in the saltwater, I had succeeded in holding onto my life vest, but it did nothing to slow my descent.

Something's not right. Something's...

Searching my body, I found no signs of being tethered to weights.

Why am I sinking? This isn't natural...

My lungs were stinging, my ears feeling the pressure from the depth. Light was fading so fast. The water was crushing in, squeezing ever harder. At last, I opened my mouth and a flood of water poured in until the black abyss filled me. My eyes squinted. *Am I in a cage?*

"When you said you were sending over supper, you didn't tell me we were having Floridians!" I could hear Captain Coomara's voice, giggling. "You've outdone yourself, Maggie."

"Well, it saves us the swim over there." It was the old woman from before! "I feel bad though. She's a sweet girl, that one."

My eyes shot open. I laid on my back in what looked to be a lobster's cage.

I know this story...

"We can keep her around for a while," offered Captain Coomara. "She's a lover of the sea... hard to eat a soul so wonderful."

Swallowing, I sat up. We were in an underwater cave, items floating in the water all around. At a table made for two there they sat, Maggie and Captain Coomara. Both of them looked different, dangerous even. Green scales twinkled in the magic of the underwater fire and danced in their pitch-black eyes. They grinned and carried on a pleasant conversation, teeth triangular and jagged. Their webbed fingers held cups of some sort of drink and from the waist down, they had fins.

Merrow. The Irish fairy tales were true. Then, this means, I'm dead, drowned, and in...

"Th-this is a soul cage, right?" I braved to make my presence known and they looked over, intrigued.

"You're a bright one." Maggie set down her cup. "You know the stories then?"

I nodded and swallowed. "I know you eat the drowned souls of sailors, fishermen and such."

"You do, now?" Captiain Coomara took a sip of his mysterious drink.

"I-I thought your name was familiar, Captain." I steadied my nerves. "It means *sea dog*, right?"

"We should keep that gal," he remarked to Maggie.

"M-may I make a request?" Swallowing, I had no pull here.

"You can try." Maggie motioned with her webbed hand.

"If you intend to keep me, that's fine. May I simply have my husband join me?" I fought the tears clawing to spill forth from my eyelids.

They broke out in a great roar of laughter. Captain Coomara slapped his knee and gasped for air. The sound of their chuckling echoing against the cave walls and vibrating through the water. Calming, he looked to Maggie and she shook her head no and nodded to him. He would be giving me my answer.

"I'm sorry, wee lass." He cleared a tear of laughter from his cold eye. "We've already ate him with our tea."

VALERIE WILLIS

Valerie Willis is a Dark Fantasy Paranormal Romance author based out of Central Florida. She loves crafting novels with elements inspired by mythology, superstitions, legends, folklore, fairy tales and history. In 2018, she received the Reader's Favorite Bronze medal in 'Fiction – Mythology' and FAPA's President's Silver medal in 'Fantasy/Sci-fi.' You can find her hosting workshops or a guest speaker at many events sharing her expertise in self-publishing, novel writing, research in fiction, worldbuilding, character development, book design, reader immersion and more.

Her Award-Winning Dark Fantasy Paranormal Romance, 'The Cedric Series,' is a wonderful blend of genres that appeal to a wide-range of readers described as "dramatic, lustful, and fantasy fulfilling." The motto here is: "No immortal is beyond the ailments of man" and that includes powerful creatures, demons, witches and Gods. Many of the monsters present in battle derive from Medieval Bestiaries and adds a fun flavor of new yet deeply rooted assortment of creatures such as Coin Iotair, Shag Foal, Cynocephali, and many more.

For Young Adult readers look for her Dark Urban Fantasy filled with coming-of-age lessons, the 'Tattooed Angels Trilogy.'

Hotan is a failed reincarnation and is becoming immortal against his will. Life is complicated and often we withdraw within ourselves and shut others out when life becomes hard. As the story unfolds we learn the importance of opening up and asking for support in all its forms even beyond friends and family. Each immortal controls powers of nature like fire and wind or elements of humanity such as fear or judgment.

You can often find this Author hosting workshops about writing and self-publishing in the Orlando, Florida area or working on the next novel. She loves to inspire other writers and creative minds. Be sure to visit her blog for some of the writing advice she has to offer. Uniquely, she brings in a perspective that has influences from Game Development and Graphic Design.

MIDSEASON FINALE

MARK ROBINSON

"**W**hat kind of holiday are you looking for, sir?"

Beneath the wall-to-wall posters of sun, sea, and sand, the skinhead smirked and flexed his England-flag-tattooed bicep. "The out of season deal."

The travel agent turned to her screen and started tapping on the keyboard. "A winter sun holiday."

"Nah, love: football season. A mate of mine told me about it."

She looked back confused and gazed up at her colleague, who had spotted the customer, and was walking over toward their desk.

"Paul." A fellow bruiser stood over the skinhead with his hand out. There was a matching tattoo inked along his inner forearm, partially obscured beneath the rolled-up shirt cuff. "I've got the package deal you're looking for."

Without turning his head, Paul asked his colleague to fetch them a couple of brews. "Milk and two, love."

She disappeared, muttering under her breath, and he took her seat at the desktop. "Good result this season?" A smile on his face.

"Relegated."

Paul sucked in air. "Happened to us last season." He smirked. "Was a good night, though."

The skinhead nodded back and brought his hands up to the desk; his knuckles were sutured, swollen, and blackened. Paul stopped tapping at the keyboard to flex his own hands; shiny healed lines criss-crossed his knuckles. "But in the meantime..."

The skinhead sat forward as Paul rotated his screen. "I can do you a fortnight in Egypt, Algeria, Syria, or Afghanistan. Any preference?"

Paul watched his customer grin, showing off the gaps between his teeth. "Afghanistan sounds good." The man nodded, flexing his bulky neck. Lumpy scar tissue had fused the skin into a line that snaked up and around the back of his bald head.

"Good choice, my friend." He hit print with the mouse, rolling back his chair to retrieve the paper from the printer drawer. "Did it last season—a fortnight in Helmand."

The customer liked the sound of that and bent over the printout as Paul passed it to him.

"You fly you out with the troops—got a deal with a couple of units, there's always a few empty seats and nobody's the wiser—plane drops you slap bang into the chaos and one of our boys will be there to escort you." There were photos on the page, bullet points beneath the war-torn pictures.

"Do we get any tools?"

Paul grinned back, getting up and taking the teas from his scowling colleague as she brought them over and slammed them down on the desk. "Of course, all that's taken care of once you get settled in." He grabbed his mug and took a giant slurp. "Got us a place over there." He nodded at the page in the customer's hand. "Right near the action but far enough away from the troops."

The customer nodded, taking hold of his mug and gulping down the scalding hot brew.

"Our boy can speak the lingo: ex-MI6, freelance now; he runs our tours, has his own personal arsenal and a couple of ladies, only an extra one-fifty," he added, tipping the skinhead a filthy wink.

The customer's mouth turned down with a nod; it all seemed too good to be true. He had a question. They always did, and it was usually a variation on a theme: "What about the beheadings?"

Paul always had just the right answers ready and waiting for the punter. "Pure propaganda, mate. Al Qaeda post them to let the world know they're still about, but in reality...hold up, I'll show you." Turning the monitor back around, he bent over the keyboard and tapped away at the letters before spinning the screen back around to his new best pal.

A beheading video buffered. Paul played a few seconds then paused it; he flicked the mouse down to another video, but before clicking on it, he told the skinhead to remember the victim's clothes, stance, and background wall. That done, he clicked on another video and skipped ahead until both were paused at exactly the same place. "See?"

The guy had no clue but kind of nodded along anyway.

"It's the same video." Paul left it a second to sink in, but the waters were pretty stagnant. He went to another site and chose a different video to prove the point. There were now three tabs open onscreen, all of them paused at exactly the same spot. Except, the common denominators were gone; the date and time had been added after the fact. "There was only ever one beheading; what they do is film it from different angles to make them look new." Pointing to the date and time at the bottom, Paul explained that these were easily added as was the voiceover.

Still not persuaded, the skinhead asked about kidnappings, ransom demands, disappearances; bad boys getting tooled up and going over there only to be outgunned and re-categorized as just another statistic that the British Government would refuse to negotiate to secure their release.

Part of his patter was to come clean with the customer; what he was offering was not the usual, off the peg, common, or garden package holiday. What he had on offer here was strictly off the books and off the record the same way bare-knuckle boxing and dog fighting used to be. What they had here was a package holiday for the more discerning traveller, so to speak; for those that wanted a bit more boom for their buck, who wanted to let off steam and get some payback. Sunday leagues were all family orientated these days. There was nothing left for the boys who wanted a little knees up afterward, a little venting of someone else's spleen at the weekend. The challenge was all but gone; it was no longer any fun to pummel a father of three whilst his wife a kids looked on. What they wanted was a fair fight.

Unfortunately, the man wasn't convinced so Paul tried a different tack. "If Helmand's too big school for you, mate, I can set you up with a cruise off the coast of Somalia?"

The skinhead didn't like the tone and Paul knew it; reverse psychology usually worked a treat with these psychos. "Do what?!" He rounded on the travel agent.

Paul sat his ground. "Somalia. If Helmand's not for you, we can take it down a notch." Maintaining eye contact, he rotated his shoulders.

"Somalia?!" He spat like the word itself tasted putrid. The man's beefy finger slammed down onto the printout of Helmand. "This is the place."

Paul lightened and cracked a smile, revealing missing teeth that were really dark caps. "Fucking-A, it's the place!"

Best of pals again. Outside, the sun was shining, shoppers wandered past the glass-fronted shop window, and the world rolled along.

They went through the paperwork and the skinhead handed over his bank card. Paul slotted it into the clone reader he always carried around with him and asked the geezer to enter his pin.

Beautiful.

Within the hour, the bruiser left the Travel Agents with the holiday of his dreams. Once the automatic door swooshed closed behind him, Paul gave up the seat and took his usual booth along the back wall of the shop. There was a rubber band bundle of post there waiting for him to go through.

Mostly circulars and bumf from head office, Paul filed it in the bin next to his seat. That was, until he came to a post-card. It was of a seascape, but the destination was obscured by what looked like dried bloodied finger prints. Paul flipped the photo over to take a read of the reverse side but dropped it down on his desk, instead.

"Another 'wish you weren't here,' Pauley?" His colleague Doug aimed for friendly, but failed. Doug stopped smiling when Paul went to get up from his desk. Doug moved on, not meeting his eyes as all his other colleagues tended to do, taking his chair at the desk farthest away from psycho Paul.

The rest of the shop knew he had something on the side but never dared to dig too deeply into his business. Like they all knew he'd been inside a while back but hadn't asked what he'd been in for. Or where the photos of his family had been moved to from the corner of his desk and why he stopped wearing his wedding ring.

The message on the postcard was the same as the others. Not like every other one he'd ever had from a customer; travel agents received dozens of them during the year and most of them were full of gratitude and thank yous from satisfied repeat customers. But it was the same as the others he'd been getting recently. In all, he'd had around six cards over the past year, all from far flung places across the globe that he'd never even heard of, let alone sent people to. Sunny pictur-esque climes with the destination partially obscured by what seemed to be dried blood and a message daubed in the same red scrawl. Paul was a big guy that didn't scare easily but every single one of these cards he received rattled him.

On the bookcase behind his desk, he pulled out a ring binder and flipped through the hole-punched plastic wallets where he'd stored the cards like evidence. Different destina-tions around the world but all of them identical: bright blue skies, bright white sandy beaches, not a soul in view. A veri-table paradise on earth. Only that's not what these were cap-turing. These 'scapes were showing him a picture of hell and the blood smears were proof of that. As were the messages posted on the reverse. All of them friendly, quirky, and jovial in tone. However, in the way that they had been written, they came across as anything but: "Kiss me quick," "Wish you were here," "I saw this and thought of you," "Keep calm and carry on."

None of these were good time greetings from a friend but warnings.

The new one, he flipped it back over and checked the postage stamp; this one had been posted in England, along the east coast somewhere.

Creasing his brow, Paul took it and those from the binder and jumped up, noting Doug flinch from the corner of his eye as he did so. That made him smile, luke-warmed that place inside where that latest postcard had cooled.

Over in the other corner of the shop, around the side of his desk, along that entire wall was a huge world map. They used it to show the customers where they were going. It also looked pretty good. Paul took a handful of drawing pins and started tacking the postcards up based on the date and where the postmark stamp said they were sent from.

Tripoli, Syria, February last year; Al Arish, Egypt, May; Surt, Libya, September; Tangiers, Morocco, December; Gijon, Spain, five months ago. And the latest one, Great Yarmouth, England. Day before yesterday.

Paul stood back, surveying his work. The postcards, now tacked up on various points of the map, could be viewed as a stepping stone or voyage. Just over a year it had taken someone to make it back to the UK. That's what it looked like to him.

Staring into the middle distance, Paul rubbed his stubbly chin. He needed to get out of here, get a bit of fresh air, go for a walk.

That's when his office phone rang.

He stared at it, the red light blinking in time with each ring. Doug was with an elderly couple, fawning over a brochure, while Becky—the woman who made him a cup of tea—was on her own extension gushing to some customer.

Paul crumpled, took one last glance at the world on the wall, and went to answer his phone. *"Happy Holidays.* Paul speaking."

Nothing but dead air.

"Hello?"

"Pauley." A low grumble, he just about heard. "You got my postcards, did you?"

It was him. The owner of the bloody fingerprints. Paul knew that voice. Plucking up an inch of courage after sending those postcards to him, anonymously, it was clear the man was just trying to scare him. The fact that it actually did unnerved Paul beyond measure.

Some wide-boy who'd gotten more than he'd bargained for, thought he was harder than he actually was; some numpty who'd balked at the first sign of trouble wanted him to know about it. Of course, the fact he'd sent a load of postcards showed he was nothing; if he'd been a real man, he wouldn't have sent cards. No, he'd simply have swaggered right into the travel agent office, pulled Paul up from his desk, and pounded him in the face.

No, whoever had sent those cards and was on the other end of this phone, was weak. Paul had this. "Postcards?" He made his voice sound like he was trying to remember. But the bloke in his ear didn't buy it.

A gruff laugh rang in his ear. "Yeah, Pauley, you got them. I know you got them."

Behind him, Doug was laughing it up with the old couple and Becky—at the other side of the shop—was talking into her phone and twirling her long hair around her finger. Paul looked from his colleagues to the world map on the wall then back to the open ring binder on his desk.

"You left me there, Pauley." The voice in his ear was almost familiar, like an actor's name on the tip of his tongue. "There was no one there to meet us, like you said there would be."

One hand held the receiver, the other his head.

"No tour guide, no place, no guns...no nothing." He said the last two words so quietly Paul almost missed them. "I almost died out there."

That was the whole point. Paul gazed down at the scars zig zagging across his knuckles. They reminded him of his father's hands. He closed his eyes, seeing his own son's small pale hands. Not a scar on them. He took a breath and opened up. "So?" He waited for the point of all this: the postcards, the phone call. "If you're looking for an apology, mate, you're in for a long wait."

Another gruff laugh in his ear. "No, that's not what I want."

Paul waited some more. Across the shop, Becky was off the phone and headed off to the little kitchenette out back next to the store room. And Doug, he'd signed the old couple up to some turkey and tinsel holiday or cruise or something and was back on that dating website.

With an exhale of air, Paul asked the man, "So, what is it you want?" Once he'd said it, though, he decided he didn't really care what the answer was. This man's time was up. It was game over. Without waiting for an answer, Paul dropped the receiver back into the cradle and leaned back into his ergonomic office chair.

After another breath, he grabbed his jacket, got up, and headed out, once again noticing that Doug flinched at the sudden movement. Leaving the postcards tacked up on the world, he swaggered out of the automatic doors and to his left.

The air was cool on his head. He'd been sweating. Paul shook it off: the tight feeling in his chest, the slight ache in his shoulders, the numpty who was trying to mess with him.

At the corner of the high street, Paul ducked into the newsagents for a pack of cigarettes. His skin feeling prickly usually meant he was low on nicotine and needed a top up. The cashier fumbled with his change, allowing Paul another smirk as he left the shop and went to find his car.

With the tip of his cigarette lit, he swaggered on along the row of parked cars until he found his.

Parked crooked on double-yellow lines, the beat-up car stood out as he fumbled to find his keys and inhaled on his coffin nail. He was out of there. Yanking the driver's door wide, he dropped inside and slammed it back before jabbing the key into the ignition, missing the first couple of times he tried.

He took a drag and growled it out. That moron had gotten to him. And nobody got to Paul.

The engine roared to life when he twisted the key.

Not waiting for shoppers to move, Paul pulled out of his space and gunned the accelerator. Sliding past the shop, he gazed across inside at Doug and Becky standing together eyeing his postcards on the wall. At the give way sign, he pushed on, pulling out into oncoming traffic without signalling and floored it until his workplace was a tiny speck in the distance.

Smoke pluming from the open window, he realized that it was well past time he had a holiday of his own. There was no reason why those postcards should have gotten to him the way they had. And that phone call? Number one, he still couldn't believe he'd picked it up. Then the fact that he'd stayed on the line as long as he did, enabling that idiot, allowing him to get into his head.

No, he needed a break. With that new card he'd cloned this morning, he'd be able to pack a bag and jump on a plane for a week or two. Recharge and refresh. Yeah, that's what he'd do; he'd go on holiday, a vacation, a long hiatus until the dust settled. Nowhere fancy, somewhere with a bit of sun to bronze himself up a little. A city by the coast, somewhere no one would notice or bother him for a while.

In less than ten minutes, he was parked outside his flat. He took another cigarette from the pack and lit it as he headed over to the main foyer. Paul's passport was in his underwear drawer. He'd empty that into a bag he kept on top of the wardrobe and head to the airport.

Through the door, he went up the stone steps—two at a time—keys still jingling in his hand right up until he reached his front door...that was standing partway open.

Paul blew a lungful of smoke at the metal number fixed at eye level to his door. He locked it this morning. Closing his eyes, Paul tried to recall that but wasn't sure whether he could. He could see himself locking the door. He'd done it hundreds of times but, this morning—what, a few hours ago—the memory wasn't there.

Paul pushed open the door and saw him, the man who sent the postcards, just sitting there at his kitchen table. "How's it going Pauley?"

He recognized the bruiser despite the leathery skin. Hearing movement behind him, feeling a shadow fall across his back, Paul glanced back. Two men, big bastards, both naturally dark-skinned, bore down on him.

"My associates," explained the man whose name Paul never even asked for back then, when he'd cloned his card and sent him away for a holiday he'd never forget.

A hand closed around each of Paul's shoulders. He flexed them under the pressure but that just made the grip tighten.

"I owe them my life." Pressure pushed Paul forward into his flat; there was no way of stopping it. To do so would be pointless and painful. As the front door eased closed behind him, Paul was told that, "In return, these men are going to take yours."

MARK ROBINSON

Hailing from the UK, Mark Robinson's short stories have appeared in over thirty publications, online and in print. These include Unlikely Stories, A Thousand Faces, and Thrillers Killers and Chillers. His first collection, International Best Cellar, can be found on Amazon. A novella entitled The Moirologist and his debut novel, Best Wishes, are currently looking for a home.

A Little Fishing Trip

Al Hagan

It was just a simple little fishing trip.
They thought.

"Jake, let's go fishing this weekend. My dad has a camp with a little house and a dock."

Paul was a laid-back Louisiana boy from Lafayette. He liked to drink beer, hunt, fish, and make low-key passes at the girls that gained him more success than the high-pressure ones.

"Uh, okay. I guess I'm not doing anything else. What do I need to bring?"

Jake was a newly-graduated petroleum engineer from Colorado and had just started his first real, adult job at a refinery in Baton Rouge, Louisiana. He figured if he was going to have a career in the oil and gas industry, then he was probably going to end up working in Louisiana and Texas and the Middle East at some point.

He was a little stiff in this new position, inclined to stick to all the rules, but that was just the new-job jitters. He might have been a little tightly wrapped, but he and Paul had quickly become friends, due almost entirely to Paul's gregariousness.

The fishing camp was in the Atchalafaya Swamp on a little spit of relatively dry land. The house was typical for South Louisiana, perched eight feet up on stilts to keep it above the frequent floods. Underneath was a patio of sorts with a sink and counter space to clean fish or ducks or whatever. Up the stairs and inside, it had a single large room and a bathroom. The room had a minimal kitchen against one wall, bunks against another wall, a dinette set, a couch, and some chairs.

"It's not luxury, but hey, it has all the comforts of home," Paul said.

With the boat in the water, they headed out to Paul's fishing spot. The swamp changed character as they went. Around the camp, the trees and hanging Spanish Moss made it shaded and close. Out farther in what Paul called the "lake," it was sunny and more open, but heavily dotted with islets and trees and stumps sticking out of the water. It all had a unique smell of water and mud and decaying vegetation.

By the end of the day, they had caught more than enough fish for a meal. Paul fried them in a propane fryer, and they ate their fill while popping the tops on a few beers. That was the main thing Jake had supplied: beer and gas money. Paul brought all of the equipment.

"Have you ever had frog legs?" Paul asked.

"I tried them once. They were kind of rubbery."

"Aw, man, you just haven't had them cooked right. Let me look and see if I still have my gig under here."

He clanged around for a minute before coming out and proudly handing the gig to Jake.

"That looks like a miniature pitchfork head on an immensely large handle," he commented, laughing.

"Aw, man! You don't know anything! Give me that before you hurt yourself." Paul took the gig back. "What we do is go out in the boat right up to the banks, shine the light, and gig frogs with this." He thrust the implement into the air a couple of times to simulate. "Come on. I need you to run the boat for me."

As they were about to cast the boat off, Paul stopped them.

"Oh, wait. I almost forgot. Let me turn the dock lights on." In seconds, he had hit the switch, and the dock blazed with light. He laughed as he got back into the boat. "Maybe I shouldn't tell on myself, but when I was 16, a dumb kid, I was late bringing the boat back. The sun went down, and I didn't even have a flashlight, trying to find the dock. My dad was in the truck, flashing the lights and blowing the horn, trying to guide me in. That's why we have all these lights on the dock now."

Jake looked around at the surrounding swamp, pitch black now that the sun was down. "Wow, I wouldn't want to be lost in there."

"It's the largest swamp in the United States. Over a million acres. If you get lost in here, you're going to stay lost. But tonight we have lights. Here's a headlamp for you. It goes on your head like a sweatband, so wherever you face is where the light goes. I'm gonna need you to pilot the boat while I'm in the front gigging frogs. Oh, and put your cell phone in the console here so it doesn't get wet if you fall overboard or anything."

"Fall overboard? That's not encouraging."

"Thing happen, you know. But get back in the boat if you do because there's gators and water moccasins—that's a snake— and things like that in the water."

"Great."

Paul laughed. "You worry too much."

———

They gigged frogs for about an hour and Jake got the hang of the boat pretty well. At one point, Paul jabbed himself in the finger with the gig while taking a frog off of it.

"Ow!" He put the gig under his arm and examined the cut. "I gigged myself." He held the wounded finger over the water and squeezed it, forcing blood to drip out.

"What are you doing?" Jake asked, surprised.

"If there's anything nasty on the gig, I'm getting it out. Like if you jab your hand with a rusty nail, the tetanus doesn't shoot all through your body immediately. It's right there in the cut, so if you bleed it a little, you can probably get the tetanus out with the blood."

Jake made a noncommittal "hmm" noise, but he was skeptical. He would have been terrified if he had known what *things* smelled the blood in the water and were coming toward them.

A few minutes later, they were close into the bank of a little islet when Jake spotted something in the reeds. He swung his light on it and received the shock of his life. His blood ran cold and hair stood up on the back of his neck.

"What is that? WHAT is THAT?" He tried to scoot back, but he was on a boat with nowhere to go.

It was the head of a girl sticking upright out of the water from the nose up. The skin was pale, fish belly white. The eyes were open—one eye, anyway, open and staring at him. The other eye was gone, the empty pit filled with writhing maggots, a single one sticking out from the mass and waving around in the air.

Paul made a guttural noise, then there was a huge splash as he went overboard. Jake threw himself across the boat to try to get to him but hesitated about sticking his hands in the water. The talk of gators and snakes had made him cautious. He could see Paul's light in the murky water, thrashing around.

He had to do something. He grabbed the paddle and thrust it down toward where he thought Paul was, to try to give him something to hold onto so he could pull him back in the boat. As soon as the paddle went into the water, a pale white arm shot up out of it and grabbed the handle, near Jake's own hands. He screamed and fell back.

Something moved in his peripheral vision, and he turned to see the girl standing up. Water sluiced off of her, and he noticed that there was some green, slimy plant caught in her hair on one side. She was wearing a bikini and a shirt with the tails tied up to leave her midriff exposed. There were horrible gashes across that midriff, arranged in an arc, as if a gator had come at her from the side and bitten down hard. Something moved inside the wounds, more maggots, or maybe the water running down her body just gave that illusion.

Jake was frozen in terror and shock until she took a step toward him. If she took two more, she could lay those wet, water-shriveled hands on him. That thought galvanized him into action. He lunged for the controls. Turning the wheel hard over, as far away from the girl as he could, he jammed the throttle to top speed.

The boat surged and slewed over to the side, and the propeller thumped on something, and then it was out in deeper water and running true. A small, distant part of Jake's mind thought that the thumps had been the propeller hitting Paul's body, but it was not something he could deal with at the moment.

He realized the route was treacherous, and he was far over-driving his light, but it took a monumental effort to pull the throttle down to a lower speed. He had never been a religious person, but he was saying "Jesus" over and over in an unending stream.

The fishing camp was really only about a mile away, and the blazing lights from the dock served as an excellent beacon, just as they were meant to do. The route zig-zagged around cypress trees and little islets of land, but Jake always knew where he was going. That distant part of his mind was thankful that he wasn't lost somewhere in the vastness of the swamp.

He ran the boat into the dock too hard, not caring about damage, and clambered out, desperate to get away from the water and the *things*. The boat tried to slip out from underneath him, and he leaped for it, falling onto the dock in a heap. It didn't matter. He jumped up and ran off the dock into the yard.

Once on dry land, he deliberately fell to his knees and almost kissed the ground. But he knew he wasn't safe yet. The girl, the *thing*, had been able to walk back there. That meant she could walk over here. He had only gotten away temporarily.

Paul! He had to call emergency services about Paul!

He reached for his phone, but his pocket was empty. He remembered putting his phone with Paul's phone in the console of the boat for safekeeping.

The boat that he hadn't tied up to the dock.

The boat that was now drifting away into the swamp.

He gave an anguished little cry and took a couple of steps toward the dock. But the boat was yards from the dock now and drifting farther out into the darkness. Drifting slowly, lazily, but opening the gap nonetheless. He wasn't going to stick one toe in that water, much less actually swim in it. The boat was in sight, but it was gone—not an option.

The truck! He ran to it, trying the door. Unlocked! But where were the keys? He dug through the console, the cup holders, frantically tossing aside change and business cards and clutter. No key fob. He stopped, glanced out at the swamp, then ran for the house. The only other places the fob could be were the console of the boat or the kitchen counter.

Please be on the counter. Please be on the counter. The litany ran through his mind, replacing the "Jesus" chant from earlier.

No keys. The counter was bare. He ripped through Paul's bed, then his overnight bag, dumping things out and pawing through them. No keys.

It dawned on him that he might not make it out of this alive. Whatever happened was going to happen here. He couldn't call anyone for help. He couldn't run away. It would be here.

He jumped up and started shoving furniture against the door.

Something started tapping on the floor from underneath. The cabin wasn't that big, but whatever was doing the tapping seemed to be able to transport from one corner of it to the other in no time. Either that, or there were more than one of them.

Taptaptap here, then *taptaptap* there, across the room, then *taptaptap* by the door, and on the door itself.

Jake snatched his feet up and fell onto the couch when the tapping happened right under his feet.

It moved on, and he stamped on the floor a couple of times.

"GO AWAY!" he screamed. "GO AWAY!"

Taptaptap. Taptaptap. Taptaptap.

Desperate, he ran to the kitchen wall and snatched up the broom. He beat it on the floor as if he was trying to kill a snake.

"STOP IT! STOP IT!" The head broke off the broom, but that just made it easier to swing. He beat against the floor, trying to hit the spots that the things were tapping, like a bizarre game of Whack-A-Mole.

The tapping got faster and faster. *Taptaptaptaptaptaptaptap*. Then it started to swirl around the floor in a circle. Jake followed it, around and around and around until he was dizzy. He staggered but continued to hit the floor, and the broom snapped.

The splintered end rebounded from the floor to stab him in the forehead. He didn't even register it as pain in his frenzied, panicked state until blood flowed down his face and into an eye. He paused for a moment, swaying unsteadily on his feet and wiping at the blood.

The tapping suddenly stopped.

He almost had time to draw a shaky breath of relief before the shrieking began. Almost.

"BLOOD! BLOOD!" The first word was in a deep baritone. The second time it started higher and raced up the scale to a pitch that could almost have shattered glass. "BLOOD! BLOOD!"

Then a whole chorus of voices screamed for his blood, and now the things clawed and pounded furiously at the floorboards. Jake fell back onto the couch again, hands to his ears, screaming "STOP IT! STOP IT!" over and over to drown out the noise.

But it didn't stop, and now the floorboards begin to pop up, came up enough for fingers to appear in the cracks.

"NOOOOOO!" He launched himself off of the couch, heading for the kitchen wall again. He jerked open the drawers in the one cabinet until he found the hammer he had noticed earlier. He turned and the floor seemed to be crawling with worms. Fingers wriggled from underneath the boards, trying to work farther into the room. Trying to push the boards up farther. Trying to get to *him*.

He sagged against the cabinet and lost control of his bladder. Then one of the boards popped up right in front of him. That galvanized him into action. He fell to his knees and pounded the board back down furiously. He frantically moved around the room on hands and knees, beating the boards down, smashing fingers and hands. They were all dead white and water-shriveled. When he hit them, they splattered swamp water and a little diluted blood.

While he was beating one hand, a board opened up beside him and long fingernails clawed his leg, opening a set of gashes. He screamed in pain and turned to smack that hand. Soon after, the same thing happened by his left hand. The thing reached in enough to grab his little finger, twist it and break the bone, and then rip it off of his hand.

Jake screamed in pain. He snatched his hand back, to fall flat on his face to the floor. Terror drove him back up, drove him to use the mangled hand again, pushing against the floor, to get his face away from the fingers.

He lost all concept of time. At some point, he saw that there was an entire arm coming into the room from under one of the beds. He shoved the bed out of the way and beat the arm and beat it and beat it . . .

Daylight.

Quiet.

No arms, no fingers, no tapping, no scratching, no screaming for his blood.

It took him a long time to begin to breathe normally. The cabin was a wreck. He had thrown the furniture around to get to trouble spots. Numerous floorboards were ajar. He had ripped his knees open and bled on the floor from the nails that were partially pushed up. His missing finger and some gashes in his leg had left more spots of blood.

But it was quiet, and sunlight streamed in through the window. That was all that mattered.

There was a knock at the door. He jumped in surprise, but it was light, and it wasn't a scratch or tap, so it couldn't be the creatures. It was just a normal human knock. He went to the door, hesitated, then pulled the furniture aside and opened it, hammer in hand.

It was Paul.

"Paul! Oh, my God. Paul!" Jake dropped the hammer and wrapped Paul up in a big bear hug.

He was soaking wet and cold. His shirt was torn up in the back, and Jake's hand touched something squishy that didn't feel like skin. His mind flashed back to when he thought the boat's propeller had run over what was probably Paul.

Jake's head snapped back to look into Paul's face. His eyes were rolled back in the sockets, showing only the whites. Paul opened his mouth and water splashed out as if from an over-turned cup.

Jake stepped back with a little cry. Paul, the *thing* that was now Paul, lurched forward and then angled off to go around him, like he was just going to go to bed, as if nothing had happened. Like *excuse me; I'm tired and I'm going to sleep now*.

Jake watched him walk by, and then there was a creak on the steps. He turned to see the girl standing there in the doorway, the bikini girl with the gator bite. She smiled as she stepped on the hammer and kicked it back behind her.

He glanced behind her, where the others were gathering.

And then coming through the door.

END

AL HAGAN

Al Hagan served a four-year tour of duty with the Marine Corps between high school and college. Following completion of his undergraduate degree, he spent a number of years in the intelligence community, working both in Washington, D.C. and in foreign countries. Between work and pleasure, he has traveled extensively and has been to four continents. He has recently retired from IT project management.

HOUSEKEEPING

ERIKA LANCE

Chuck pulled his trailer into the Two Cactus Motel, right off highway 10 near Akela, New Mexico. He had been driving almost twelve hours, and he knew the next weigh station was only fifteen miles ahead on the highway.

He could not get another violation without being put on suspension. The company could not take another hit without lowering their safety rating, and that meant that he would not be paid for at least a month. It was not worth the risk.

This was the first time he had stopped in Akela. Although he had used highway 10 for most of his trips, he had the "usual" places he liked to stop or would simply pull into a rest stop. As a trucker, it was cheaper to not make a habit of staying at motels, even the cheap ones. It cut into the profit from the trip as most companies never compensated for it.

The Two Cactus Motel was a one story, u-shaped motel. It had places to park in front of the rooms and a gravel driveway that led to the back where it had room for about ten trailers if the drivers were willing to park pretty close. Chuck only saw one other truck as he turned off the engine and jumped out of the cab onto the gravel, hearing it crunch under his feet.

The first thing that hit him was how hot and dry the air was. It was over one-hundred degrees, and the wind pulled it past his skin in a way that it felt almost like sandpaper. He had to close his mouth, or he was tasting the dirt being kicked up.

As he walked around to the front of the building, he noticed that near the front was a small area that was fenced off. It had a pool that looked like it had not had any water in it for some time and two large cactuses that looked like they had grown apart from one root.

The paint on the building was a faded green with white accents. As he walked toward the office, he noticed that there were only two other cars in the lot. It was early afternoon; if this was mainly a place people would stay while passing through, then the lot would not fill up until almost sunset.

Before he walked into the office, he looked up and down the road, spotting a diner to the west just beyond the only apparent gas station at this stop. He would grab his room key and head there for an early dinner.

Walking into the office, he expected to be hit with a blast of cooler air, but instead it was only a little less warm than outside. The air was also almost sticky, and it smelled of wetness like a carpet that was cleaned and not fully dry.

There were two low dark green vinyl chairs with a table between them. There were a couple travel brochures that look like they were dated in the eighties.

A long counter took up the other half of the room, and it had a door behind it that was closed. He walked up to the counter where there was a bell.

He rang the bell twice and looked over the counter to see a paper ledger book and an older beige rotary phone that looked like it had darkened with age. After a few moments, the door behind the counter opened, and a young attractive female in her mid-twenties stepped out.

"Welcome to the two c's motel. How can I help you today?" Her voice had a southern twang to it.

"I was looking for a room for the night," Chuck said as she smiled at him.

"That is something we can arrange," she said with a wink.

Flipping back and forth through the ledger for a moment while biting at her lower lip a little, she finally placed her finger on the page and said, "I think you can take room 13."

When these words left her lips, a shiver went up his spine, and he looked around to see if there was an air conditioner just turned on.

Before he could say anything, she put the book on the counter and spun it around to face him. "I just need your full name, license plate number, and for you to sign her." She gestured to each part of the page as she spoke the words and placed a pen on the book.

"What is the cost for the room?" Chuck was debating if sleeping in the cab may be a better idea when she said, "It's twenty-five for the night." Her smile was unwavering.

He grabbed the pen and added the information to the book, then pulled the cash from his wallet and placed it on the counter. She picked it up and placed a key on the counter. "If you need anything, let me know and hope you enjoy your stay."

Chuck nodded, grabbing the key. "Thank you."

As he walked outside, he felt the sting of the wind whipping around again, and he felt more awake than he had moments ago. Looking back toward the office, he saw the girl was gone again. Shrugging, he began walking toward the diner.

He pushed the diner door open. As the cool air swirled around him, he felt the tension he had not realized he was holding in his shoulders ease. He found a booth to sit in. A waitress walked up to him, bringing a large glass of ice water and handing him a menu.

"Hello, sweetie. I will let you take a look at the menu. Our special today is a Salisbury steak, potatoes, and veggies. What would you like to drink?" She was distantly friendly in the way that most truck stop diner waitstaff were. Almost all of them he had met seemed like they were somehow stuck in the little world where the diner was. If you spent any appreciable time in these towns, you would wonder how anyone decided that the town was enough life for them to live at all.

"Coke," he replied. She nodded and walked away.

He looked over the menu for a minute, not for the food—he had already decided what he was going to have—but to see if they listed the pie options. Finding diner pie to be some of the absolute best you can find, it was something he looked forward to at each stop. Not finding any mention of the flavors, he set it down again and looked out the window at the gas station across the street.

"Did you decide what you wanted?" The waitress startled him slightly as she set down a large soda and a straw that she pulled from her apron.

"Yes, ma'am. Can I have a burger, well done, with everything and a side of fries?" She nodded, scribbling on her pad. "Also, what kind of pie do you have?"

"Apple," she replied.

"Just apple?" he asked, although as the words left his lips, he realized it was a stupid question.

"Yes, just apple." She smiled as if he had stated something that should be painfully obvious. He continued to simply look at her until she finally offered, "We do have some various ice-cream sundaes. Most people want to cool off when they come in from the heat."

"How about a piece of that apple pie and a scoop of ice-cream after the burger?" He smiled up at her without anything but annoyance behind it. She was not working on getting a good tip.

She nodded, jotting on her pad again, and told him to holler if he needed anything else.

Pulling out his phone, he scanned his email, read some news, and played a few games until the food came out. When she put the plate in front of him, it smelled amazing, and he dove in. As promised when he had taken his final bite, the waitress brought him over a piece of pie with the scoop of ice cream on top which had already begun to melt.

"Let me know if you need anything else," she said, placing his check on the table. Her shift must be ending because the check on the table was a server's way of telling you to wrap it up as soon as possible.

Taking the first bite of the pie and ice cream, he savored the wonderful taste. The fact that apple was all they had might have been a sign that it would be terrible. Instead, it was the perfect warm filling and cold cream. As he ate, he felt the stress of eating every bite he picked up his check, leaving five on the table.

Walking back to the motel, he made his way to the truck, grabbing his bag, so he could shower and change clothes. No additional trucks had joined his in the back lot. Walking past the one that he had seen on his way in, he noticed that there was a layer of dirt and dust on the truck as if it hadn't moved in some time.

As he rounded the corner to the front parking lot, it was the same. The cars he saw earlier were the only ones there. There was a layer of dirt on the cars as well. It had been a while since someone had driven any of them.

Making his way to his room, he pulled out the key, unlocking the door. Pushing the door swung open, he was happy to be greeted by cool air. He flipped the switch next to the door, which turned on the floor lamp behind a chair in the corner.

Feeling very full he set his bag down on the chair, pulled out his toiletry bag, boxers, and a clean t-shirt. He then stripped off his shoes and clothes, leaving them in a pile.

The shower was hot, and he let the water run down him for some time. The one thing he could say was a benefit for most motel rooms was that the hot water rarely ran out.

Finishing drying off, he changed into his clean shirt and boxers. He plugged in his phone next to the bed at the closest outlet, set the alarm, grabbed the remote, and got under the covers. The sheets were cool against his skin which was perfect. Turning the TV on, he found reruns of the A-Team.

It was not long before his eyes closed.

A faint sound penetrated his rest. It was a five-tone jingle that seemed to be on repeat. His eyes slowly opened as the noise got louder.

The alarm on his phone continued to blare as he grabbed for it off the nightstand. Moving to turn it off, he saw the time on his phone was 2pm. He closed his eyes and opened them again. The phone still said 2pm.

Pulling the blanket off and sitting on the edge of the bed, his skin felt sticky as if he had been sweating as he slept. The air however was still as cool as it had been when he went to bed.

Standing up, he wondered if he was just more tired than he thought he was. Sometimes when he came off the road, he would find himself sleeping for a couple of days. It was late, but if he got himself ready, now he would be able to make up the time. He was rested now. It shouldn't be too terrible as long as the weather held.

In the bathroom, he debated taking a shower but that would take up more of his time. As he was brushing his teeth, he heard a knock at the door and a muffled voice say "Housekeeping."

Spitting out the toothpaste, he replied, "Coming" and then turned on the facet to scoop some water in his mouth and noticed a couple of red spots on his hand. He rinsed and spit, then grabbed a towel to wipe his face as he arrived at the door opening it slightly.

Standing at the door with an arm full of towels was the same person he had met at the front desk the day before.

"Hi," he stumbled a bit. "I am sure I missed checkout. I, uh, overslept. I will be getting out of your hair in five minutes though, I promise."

She smiled and held the towels out to him "You can stay as long as you need, sweetie."

He took the towels with one hand, trying not to have the door open too much to reveal he still did not have pants on.

"Thanks," he said, and shivers went down his spine. Although she was smiling at him, he did not feel any warmth from it.

Several seconds passed, and he finally said, "Thanks again for the towels" and closed the door, instinctively locking it behind him.

Getting dressed, he noticed some further spots on his legs and arms. He had experienced bed bugs once in Ohio. He was hoping this was just fleas or mosquitoes.

As he slung the bag over his shoulder, he grabbed his phone and keys and headed toward the front desk. He hoped there was a key drop but found no such luck.

Entering the office, he noticed the smell had changed. No longer sickly, but more sweet and inviting. He put the key on the counter and rang the bell.

The door immediately opened, and she greeted him with the same smile.

"What do I owe you for the late departure?" He reached for his wallet.

"Nothing." Her smile widened "You have given us all you needed to." She took the key from the counter.

"Thanks again for staying with us," she said and went back into the office, closing the door.

Chuck went to his truck. He put his bag in the cab and started the engine, debating where to stop to fill up. The one thing he knew was he wanted to get distance from this place. He absently started to scratch the spots that began itching until something bit his fingertip. He looked down to find a drop of blood on his finger.

He woke up to the faint sound of water trickling in the distance. Blinking his eyes, he tried to get them to adjust, but he was in complete darkness. Moving his hands around, he felt that he was laying on a soft moist surface.

Where in the hell am I?

The last thing he remembered was leaving the motel. Had he been in a crash? Was he in a hospital?

He felt above him, and there was nothing, so he decided to try to sit up. His limbs felt heavy, and as he moved, he felt movement within him.

"Hello?" he said, trying to determine if there was anyone in the room with him. If this was a room.

"You're awake," he heard a familiar voice say.

"Where am I?"

"You're home," the voice purred.

"Home? What are you talking about?" His voice sounded almost panicked, and he felt almost vibrations under parts of his skin.

A hand on his shoulder guided him to lay back down. "Calm."

He let himself be laid back down.

"It is almost done," the voice purred, "then you can rest."

"What's almost done?" He found himself trying to stay awake again.

"The babies, of course."

ERIKA LANCE

Erika had the unique opportunity to live in several different environments across the country growing up, giving her a colorful perspective on life. Born in Minnesota, she spent most of her formative years in Hollywood, then a ranch in New Mexico on the border of an Indian reservation. With a love of the arts since she was a child (acting, painting, sewing and dancing to name a few!) she found her passion in writing. Beginning with short stories, poems and articles for local papers, "Jimmy" is her first published fiction story.

VENDING MACHINE CANDY

GEORGIA COOK

A dam opened his eyes. The back seat was dark and hazy, lit only by the reflective glow of the car's headlights off the road ahead. Adam blinked and rubbed his eyes, forcing away the miasma of sleep. "Where are we?" he asked, levering himself up into a sitting position.

The headlamp glow illuminated his parents' silhouettes in the front seat. Adam's father was bent over a map, muttering to himself. His mother was driving, her silhouette tense and straight-backed. Neither of them was speaking.

Adam's father shot him a weary glance. "Not long now, champ," he said, pushing his glasses up his nose. "Just a coupla' miles until we find a motel."

"Another motel?" Adam sat up excitedly.

"Don't tell him that!" hissed Adam's mother.

"We're not getting to your sister's tonight, Rachael," Adam's father snapped. Adam's mother rolled her eyes.

They'd been driving for what felt like weeks, but in reality couldn't have been more than a few days, the landscape rolling out ahead of them in an endless collection of motels and sleepy desert towns, punctuated by the ever-present expanse of sun-swept mountains.

"D'you think this one'll have a pool?" asked Adam. Adam's parents had forbidden him from swimming in any of the motel pools, but Adam enjoyed the thrill of knowing it was out there, just meters from their room, shimmering blue and murky green under the security lights. He imagined sneaking outside late at night to stare into the depths, watching the steam rise from the water in foggy puffs.

"Maybe, Champ." Adam's father gave him a weary smile.

Adam didn't understand why his parents looked so tired all the time. At ten years old, he'd never experienced anything as wondrous as the vast flat landscape between Home and Aunt Perry. It was an alien place, a fantastical place, ripe for exploration. As far as he was concerned, there was nothing better.

Adam settled down again, letting the movement of the car lull him into a gentle half sleep. His stomach gurgled. They'd stopped for dinner at an all-night diner several hours ago, eating half-cold burgers and sipping lukewarm soda in silence on greasy plastic chairs, Adam's mother drinking cup after cup of steaming black coffee. Now the burger lay heavy in the pit of Adam's stomach, barely enough to fill the hole.

"I'm hungry..."

"We can eat when we get there," said his father.

"Promise?"

"Sure."

Satisfied with this, Adam let the car rock him all the way to sleep.

"—didn't see this one on the map."

"Then it's new, or it's bloody cheap. Plenty of places out here aren't on the map, Mike."

"Look, I'm just saying it's odd."

The sound of his parent's voices jolted Adam awake. The car was stationary. What little Adam could see of the night sky from his position across the seats was spotted with distant stars.

"Do *you* want to keep driving?" snapped his mother. "Because you're perfectly welcome."

Adam yawned, blinking away the dregs of sleep. "Where are we?" he mumbled.

"Hey, buddy." Adam's father shot him a thin little smile across the seats.

They were parked in the tiny parking lot of a roadside motel. It might have been midnight, might have been later; the night outside was just as black as when Adam had fallen asleep. A tall metal sign overhead bore the legend "Hotel Boone" in flickering blue neon.

Adam's eyes widened in delight. *Another motel!*

"Can I have a look?"

"Now you've got him excited," snapped Adam's mother.

"At least the poor kid has something to be excited about," his father retorted.

Adam was only half listening; he was too busy staring out at the parking lot.

They bundled out of the car. Mosquitoes buzzed in the air, lured by the flickering glow of the motel sign. The air was thick with a dry desert heat. Behind the parking lot gates, the landscape stretched on and on into flat oblivion, lit only by a sprinkling of stars and the orange tinge of light pollution.

The motel itself occupied a low squat building, built in a square horse-shoe shape around the parking lot. It rose to only two floors, the upper floor ringed by a rickety metal guard rail, offering views across the night-black desert.

To Adam's disappointment, he couldn't see a pool. "Can we get a room up there?" he asked, pointing.

"We'll get whatever room they give us, champ," said his father.

"I want to see the view."

"Won't be much of a view out here."

"There might be."

"This is what we get for stopping in the middle of nowhere," muttered his mother. Adam's father said nothing.

There were several other cars in the parking lot, their sides and windows thick with dust. While his parents' backs were turned, Adam swept his hand across the window of the nearest one. It came away gray, the smear left by his palm revealing nothing inside but darkness. Adam giggled, wondering how long he'd have to stay in a place like this to turn gray with dust.

"Adam!" snapped his mother. His parents had arrived at the doors to the reception, their tired silhouettes backlit by the flickering yellow light coming from within. Wiping his hand hurriedly on his trouser leg, Adam ran to catch up.

The hotel reception was a long, narrow room, presided over by a tiny alcove in the wall by the door, containing a desk and a smiling young woman. The air smelled of dust and old mold, shot through with the back-of-the-throat tinge of disinfectant. The walls were covered in a dull beige wallpaper. Thin brown carpet crunched underfoot. Several watercolor prints of stylized desert scenes hung crooked on the wall behind the reception desk.

"It's like a throwback from the fucking 70's," muttered Adam's mother. Adam's father shushed her.

The smiling young woman greeted them from behind the desk. She was dressed in a crumpled blue shirt and jeans, her hair swept back from her forehead with a butterfly clip. The name on her name tag said "Kate Boone."

"Welcome to the Hotel Boone," she said. "Do you have a reservation?"

"No, sorry." Adam's father flashed the woman a tired smile. "Do you have any free rooms?"

"Of course, they do," muttered Adam's mother. "*Look* at this place."

The girl didn't appear to hear her. "I'll just check—"

Kicking his heels, Adam stared around the tiny space. An ancient vending machine stood in a far corner, its inner cabinet illuminated by a flickering neon glow. The welcoming shapes of candy bars and bottles of soda sat in neat orderly rows.

Adam's stomach growled again, louder and more insistent than it had in the car. "Mom…"

"Later, Adam."

The woman returned with a set of jangling room keys. "Room 15's free?" she said.

Adam's father nodded gratefully. "Perfect. *Anything.*"

Adam gazed longingly at the vending machine as his father paid for the room, but neither of his parents paid it any attention as they wheeled their bags across the reception and into the motel corridors.

To Adam's disappointment, their room was on the ground floor, near the reception. It was a cramped one-bed affair, almost identical to the five motels they'd already encountered on their road trip; there was a couch and a battered chest of drawers and a rickety desk bearing the weight of a flickering black-and-white TV. A crooked ceiling fan shifted the dusty air back and forth, making no difference at all to the desert heat.

Adam sat on the mattress, swinging his legs, while his mother made a bed for him on the tiny couch. He wasn't tired anymore, but he didn't dare tell his parents; they were too busy playing their usual game of studiously ignoring one another. His stomach gurgled again.

The couch was hard and uncomfortable. A sharp lump prodded the small of Adam's back, painful no matter which way he turned. The neon glow of the sign outside filtered through the gossamer-thin curtains, casting the world in a haze of almost-blue.

Adam stared at the ceiling, too hungry to sleep, too hot to move. He pictured the vending machine, tall and inviting out in reception. His stomach growled. A thought arose, terrible and daring:

How difficult would it be to sneak outside and have a look? Not buy anything, but just...look?

His parents would never have to know.

Slowly, slowly, Adam sat up.

The ceiling fan turned lazily overhead. His parents' sleeping forms lay silent in the narrow double bed next to him, turned away from one another in the stifling gloom. Neither of them stirred. Adam watched his father's chest rise and fall.

The little digital clock on the bedside table flashed 3am, the side of midnight when night time became an alien world. Adam had become accustomed to strange hours and long drives, but still he marvelled at the silent thrill of being up so late.

A second thought joined the first, just as terrible, just as daring:

...a candy bar wouldn't cost much, would it? Just a few dollars, and then I'll be right back.

His parents would never know. And he'd pay them back as soon as he got his allowance.

Adam shifted back the blankets as quietly as he could, dropping to the floor without a sound. Although the room was dark, the neon glow through the curtains was just enough to guide him through the treacherous path of furniture and belongings.

Fumbling in the gloom, Adam found his mother's bag on the floor by the desk and prised it open. Forcing down a twinge of guilt, he selected a handful of dollar bills from his mother's purse, stuffed them inside his pajama pocket, and hurried to the door. It opened with a slow creak, letting in a sliver of almost-light from the corridor. Adam cast a glance over his shoulder, but neither of his parents had stirred. He held his breath, steeled himself, and slipped outside.

The world was quiet. The corridor stretched on in both directions, row after row of identical doors. Nothing moved in the surrounding rooms: no footsteps, no murmur of distant voices. Adam wondered idly who else was staying here at the motel; presumably whoever had let their cars get so dusty in the parking lot outside. Were they all traveling somewhere, like Adam and his parents?

The young woman was gone from behind the reception desk as Adam made his way into the lobby. The lights were dimmed. A new smell hung in the air, mingling with the disinfectant and dust—like spoiled meat and leaf mold.

Adam turned toward the welcome glow of the vending machine—

But someone was already there.

A man stood with his back to Adam, peering into the cabinet with an expression of concentrated interest. He was tall and thin, dressed in black, with long bony fingers and the palest skin Adam had ever seen. He was leaning on a long black walking stick, bending to inspect the soft drinks.

Adam stood and watched him a moment, wondering if he would move. "Hello," he said at last, reluctantly.

The man turned. His face was narrow and bony and completely hairless with deep-set eyes and sharp cheekbones. If he was surprised to see Adam there, he didn't show it.

"Hello," he replied. He had a low, whispering voice—was he ill?

The wedge of dollar bills felt heavy in Adam's pocket. Would the man spot them? Would he know they were stolen? Would he tell Adam's parents? "What are you looking for?" he asked, in case it might distract the man from asking about his pockets.

The man smiled, his gaze returning to the machine cabinet. "On nights such as this, occasionally I like to...indulge."

Adam nodded; adults said weird things like that sometimes. "Did you get here late too?" he asked.

"I never arrive late."

"Oh." Adam shifted uncomfortably. "It's a nice place for a holiday." Adam had always been told to be polite to adults, even weird adults.

The man chuckled. "I don't take holidays," he said, still examining the cabinet. "Should I attempt the soda pop or the sweet candy, do you think?"

Adam stood aghast at this. No holidays? His stomach prickled with indignation. "None at all?" he asked.

"The candy, I think." A long finger tapped a code into the vending machine control panel. It gave a beep of acknowledgement. A mechanism deep within the machine began to whirr, sputtering and whining with the effort, before finally dropping a candy bar neatly into the tray at the bottom. The strange man bent to retrieve it. "Regrettably, my work is often in high demand." He shot Adam another glance. "I am on a work trip."

"Oh." Adam knew about those; occasionally his father would take long working trips across the country, leaving Adam and his mother for weeks at a time. Adam's mother would laugh about that, although Adam never understood the joke. "We're going to visit my Aunt."

"I see."

"She lives in Florida."

"What a regrettable distance."

"That's what my Mom says." Adam shuffled awkwardly. The candy bar glistened in the man's pale hand, unopened. Adam wished he would move away from the vending machine. "Do you own one of the cars outside?"

"I do not."

"Then how did you get here?"

"Sometimes I find it best to...hang around. Arrive early, as it were."

"So, you work here?"

The man seemed to find this immensely amusing. "Sometimes, yes. I suppose I do. I've worked in this region for a very long time. But for now, I am merely...waiting."

"Waiting for what?"

The man merely smiled. Above his head, one of the ancient fluorescent light bulbs began to flicker—not much, just enough to notice. "This place is very old. Did you know that?"

"My mom said it looked like something from the 70's." Adam didn't quite know what that meant, but 70 was an impressively large number.

"Did she now? An astute woman." The man smiled. "It's older than that. It has had many names."

"Like what?"

The man didn't answer. Instead, he turned and stared across the hotel lobby, out through the windows into the night-black parking lot. "Have you ever heard of the Bender family?" he asked suddenly.

Adam shook his head.

"The Kellys?"

Again, Adam hadn't.

"Such a pity," sighed the man. "Such dedicated craftsmen. How soon the young forget."

"Who were they?"

The man shrugged. "Cannibals. Bandits. Desert spirits. Waiting to catch and consume the unwary. They stalked this beautiful desolate landscape in the guise of a charming little Inn, I believe. This was hundreds of years ago, of course—how quickly times change."

Adam drew back. "I don't like that story."

The man smiled wider. His teeth were very straight, Adam noted, and very white. In the luminous glow of the vending machine, his black coat seemed to change—grow longer, darker, older, until it appeared, for just a second, that the man was wearing a piece of pitch-black night draped around his shoulders.

"It's an old story," he said as the bulb above their heads began to flicker again. "A very old story, attracted to all the lonely little places in the world, shifting and twisting beneath the high black sky. Every desolate road must have a ghoul. Every patch of darkness must hold a ghost story. And some-where, just somewhere, one lovely little inn must have a kitchen filled with blood."

Now Adam was uneasy. As well as being polite to adults, he'd also been warned never to talk to strangers—a contra-diction of advice that had always puzzled him, but now began to make a terrible kind of sense.

"But those stories aren't true," he whispered in what he hoped was a good impression of his mother. "Those things aren't real."

The man simply smiled. Above him, the flickering bulb cast strangely distorted shadows across the back wall, making it seem as if his walking stick had sprung a long curved blade at the handle. "I do so enjoy talking to the young," he said, in a voice like rushing sand. "So much optimism. Such bound-less faith." He straightened suddenly. "But now, I think, it is time to return to work."

The man held out a hand. Adam flinched, before recognizing the brightly coloured plastic of the candy bar. Cautiously, his hands trembling, Adam reached out and took it. It was ice cold.

"For the return trip," said the man.

Adam stumbled back to his room, his heart pounding, the candy bar clutched to his chest. He could feel the thin plastic wrapper through his pajamas, ice cold despite the desert heat.

The motel corridor was warm and silent. No sounds of TV static from behind the rows of doors, no shuffling feet or muffled coughing. For the first time in his life, Adam became acutely aware of his own isolation: an absolute Aloneness.

Up ahead, his parent's door hung ajar. Adam froze in horror—he'd left it open! His parents were going to kill him! He shuffled forward nervously, waiting at any moment for his mother's voice to cut through the air, for the weight of his father's hand on his shoulder. The bedroom light was off, leaving a sliver of darkness beyond the door.

Nothing stirred. Nothing moved.

Adam sniffed. The same coppery smell from the lobby hung in the air, like wet meat, or stale hamburgers. The candy bar crinkled in his hand, already growing hot and squishy. Adam peered into the gloom. Just beyond the light of the hallway, a black stain glistened across the carpet. Had someone spilled a drink? Had his parents discovered him missing, and were now waiting up to scold him?

The smell was thicker now. Almost choking.

"Hello?" Adam whispered, feeling suddenly very small and afraid. "Hello?"

Nothing answered.

Slowly, slowly, Adam eased open the door.

GEORGIA COOK

Georgia Cook is an illustrator and writer from London, specialising in folklore and ghost stories. She is the winner of the LISP 2020 Flash Fiction Prize, and has been shortlisted for the Bridport Prize, Staunch Book Prize and Reflex Fiction Award, among others. She can be found on twitter at @georgiacooked and on her website at https://www.georgiacookwriter.com/

WHEN THE MUSIC STOPS

MARK TOWSE

The scent of sweet human flesh carries on the autumn breeze, bringing the first hunter from its pit. The smell is getting stronger, tantalizingly so. Two of them, *it* surmises, one of them a youngling. Taking another long sniff, it begins moving between the trees, following the scent and getting ready to alert the others. Not yet. Sunlight works in favor of humans, but time will take care of that.

"Dad, wait!"

Ethan felt much more comfortable lagging behind on the path, but now they're trudging through meaner undergrowth that shows a hunger for his shoes, he's keen to be back within sniffing distance of his dad's aftershave. "Dad, wait up!" A short burst takes him closer, but his father is on a mission, backpack swinging violently and arms pendulously cutting through the air.

"Not much farther, kiddo!"

The expression no longer carries any weight, certainly a case of cry wolf used on too many road trips to count. "Fifteen minutes, tops," his dad said, but already twenty have passed. He opens his mouth to gripe but remembers the look in his father's eyes when he asked if he could stay by the fire.

Instead, he zips up his jacket and performs another sprint, searching the ever-thickening canopy for the sinking sun. The forest smells different, damper and heavier, and the growing tapestry on the meshy carpet of green means they're more often than not walking through shadows. He lets out a shiver as he reaches his father's side. "Do you think we'll find it?"

"Absolutely." Jack shows off the compass on his iPhone display. "Tech isn't just for kids, you know. Just got to keep heading dead north."

"It's been years, though."

"Above ground, everything moves so fast, Eth, but down there, not so much." Jack offers his son a wink and a ruffle of his hair, noting the screwed-up face of disdain. "Point proven."

Sometimes Ethan doesn't understand his dad; there's a divide, unlike with his mum. "You need to go with him; it means a lot," she said to him by the fire. "Your dad was so excited when he found out we were having a boy. He cried, you know; loves you to the moon and back."

"How come Mum and Sis got to stay at camp?"

Jack looks at the ground and lets out a sigh. "Do you remember the happiest day of your life?"

Ethan considers the question for a moment. "I reckon it was Christmas before last—PlayStation four."

"Not quite the emotional punch I was hoping for, Eth, but yeah, I get it."

"Actually, no. Can I change that to the first time I beat you at Call of Duty?"

Jack nods and smiles. "I had the trip planned with Pete for ages, booked for over a year. Even though your mum was pregnant, she insisted I follow through. Best friends on an eight-day hike into the lush Tasmanian forest. No work, no timetable, no distractions. Yet the entire time, all I could think about was the fact I would soon be a father, that I would have a son. I guess I just wanted to immortalize that feeling of utter happiness."

"Huh?"

"Make it last forever. So, I wrote a letter to you, hoping that we would return together one day and dig it up. And here we are." He turns to Ethan, his face splitting into a smile. "Son."

He allows his dad's arms to slide across his shoulders without a fight. "Can you remember what you wrote?"

"Vaguely. Something about wishing Celtic would win the premiership."

Shaking his head and wrinkling his nose, Ethan eventually looks up to his father for clarity. The wink and awaiting smile say it all, but at least he doesn't get the ruffle treatment again.

"Used my spare tartan flask and buried it in the ground about two feet deep. To its right is a rock that Pete named The Screaming Stone. You'll know why when you see it."

Ethan lets out a shudder, wishing he was back by the fire sipping on a mug of hot chocolate. Light is fading, and it feels like the temperature has halved in the last few minutes. Matching his father stride for stride, he eyes the skeletal trees, certain he'll find something glaring back.

Its sticky tendrils stretch out like branches, and its slimy and leathery body stands upright and motionless. Snout pointing to the sky is not its natural position, and it's becoming more than a strain. Sunlight burns its eyes, too, but it has to eat. Moving only when the humans do, *it* knows they are faster and see better in daylight, but darkness will take that edge away. For now, it smells and listens. And waits.

Jack affords himself a smile of relief. "There!" It took longer than he remembered, but he and Pete were always competitively trying to outpace each other.

His dad's cry draws his attention away from *it* and toward the eerie-looking rock that makes for the most sinister of landmarks. Resembling four stretched faces frozen in a mid-terror scream, it suits the name perfectly and sends a shudder down Ethan's spine. His digital watch tells him they're only thirty minutes from camp, but it's as though they've ventured into another realm, the dark side of the forest that nurtures strangeness—the stuff of nightmares.

"Told you it wasn't far." Jack crouches and runs his fingers across the soil. "It's as if it was yesterday."

But Ethan's attention is elsewhere. Did he really just see that? To his right, orbs of light dart between the trees. He holds onto his breath, watching, waiting.

"Dad, I think—"

There—again—the yellow! But he blinks, and they're gone again.

"Dad."

It feels even colder now they're still, the biting wind wrapping around his neck. Darker, too, as if stopping has allowed time to move ahead of them.

"Dad, I think there's something in the forest."

Jack shrugs off his backpack and reaches inside. "Lots of things in the forest, son." He brings out the trowel and skims off the surface layer. "Rabbits, wallabies, all sorts of little critters."

Ethan put it down to floaters before, but the recent glimpses of light were more vivid, two perfectly defined spheres floating impossibly high above the ground. Not rabbits or wallabies. He squints into the darkness, eyes fixed on the smaller trunk again, its branches perfectly still against the cutting wind, in contrast to the larger ones that give to its power.

"Eth," Jack mumbles. "Look at this, Eth."

Not taking his stare away from the tree, Ethan begins slowly backing up, relieved for his father's aftershave to be permeating the air once more. Briefly, he glances toward the object on display but quickly averts his gaze back into the bowels of the forest. He's sure that tree is closer than before.

"I think it's bone," Jack says. "I would have said jaw, but these—these throw me." He runs his finger up and down the broken tube-like appendages as if he was David Attenborough, not an accountant with a penchant for the occasional hike.

Ethan pinches hard at the flesh just below the elbow of his left arm, his go-to spot when at the dentist. The knot in his stomach tightens further as he searches for the sun without success. "I want to call Mum."

"Why?"

"I just want to speak to her."

"I'd rather she didn't worry for no reason, Eth. We'll be on our way back in a few minutes." Jack opts to leave out the lack of signal, knowing it could be a trigger. He puts the piece of bone in his pocket and hurriedly sloshes some water across the dirt.

The humans' scent is overwhelming. It has to be done right, though, or it could all be for nothing. Slowly, it begins exhaling through its snout, the exaggerated note carrying on the wind and alerting the others to their presence, but also its claim.

"Hear that?" Ethan's hairs bristle on the back of his neck, and he gives out another shudder. It sounded close.

Jack nods. "Owl, maybe?" As he begins stabbing at the ground with the trowel, another whistle floats across, distant this time. "Beautiful," he comments as he scrapes more earth into the growing pile. "They must be calling to each other."

"Have you got it?"

"Not much more to go, kiddo."

A slight variation on "Not much farther" but no more satisfying. Ethan grabs the small torch from his back pocket and cuts the beam across the darkness. *That was no fucking owl.*

"Watch my eyes, bud."

"Sorry!"

Another whistling sound emerges, this one from up close again. He directs the light toward the source, and it lands on that same tree, the slightly smaller one that stands too still for Ethan's liking. He swings the torch to the right as another whistle cuts through the silence. To the left. Behind. His heart quickens with each haunting note, and he curses his mum for letting her talk him into this.

"I don't understand. It should be right here."

"Can we go now?"

"Ethan, this was the whole purpose of the trip. Please don't start with your whining."

"I'm not whining. But the noises are—"

"Ethan, stop!" Jack scans the ground, forehead creased, eventually starting to hack again at the hole already created. "Must be deeper," he mumbles.

Biting down hard on his lip and squeezing at his arm, Ethan tries to stay brave, but he's sure he catches sight of more streaks of yellow in the distance. "Dad." He spins around again toward another whistle, convincing himself he sees shadows moving within the shadows.

"Come on. It has to be—"

"Dad!" Ethan bellows, attempting to follow the sounds with the beam.

"It's gone. Someone must have—"

"For fuck's sake, listen, will you!"

Jack gets to his feet, mouth agape at witnessing his son's first f-bomb. Instead of scolding, though, he begins snapping his head toward the sounds that are getting noticeably frequent. He opens his mouth to speak, usually with an answer for everything, but nothing comes to mind. This is "twilight zone stuff," as Melissa would say. He catches the strap of the backpack and hoists it up, beginning his search, but cussing as he remembers the late-night bowel movement, knowing the torch will be waiting for him under his pillow when they get back.

"They're getting louder, closer." Ethan works at his zip but can't get it any higher. "Dad, can we go now?" As he speaks, wisps of cloud emerge from his mouth. Too many changes to deal with in a short space of time. "I really think there's something out there."

Jack weaves his arms through the pack and offers a nod. "Probably best. Your mother will freak if we're not back soon." He habitually strokes his chin and lifts the phone, setting off south, past The Screaming Stone. "Light us up, son."

The soundtrack that plays is now continuous, an unbroken series of undulating and otherworldly whistles that prompts a layer of goosebumps across Ethan's skin. The source is impossible to pinpoint, each of the notes distant but perfectly in time and harmoniously complementing the last.

Their pace is quicker than before, their path lit by a narrow beam that occasionally flickers off toward the trees and filtered moonlight that squeezes its way through.

"Keep it straight, Eth," Jack says softly.

The song is in Ethan's head; each note beautiful yet somehow terrifying, like the tune from Nana's music box. He saw a movie about one once; something about when the dancer stopped, and the music ceased, bad things would appear in the mirror. It kept him awake for weeks.

"You alright, Eth? We'll be home soon."

It's getting louder all the time, though, closing in around them. He's trying to stay brave for his dad, but the ominous dread that continues to manifest in his chest also brings pressure behind the eyes. He can't remember ever feeling so scared. Each rustle of branches sends him into a panic, every scamper of feet. And that music in the background! He ducks beneath an offshoot, grimacing as crustiness wraps around his head, unable to stem the tears. Frantically, he begins clawing at his face and hair.

"Eth. Eth, it's just a cobweb. Here, look at me."

It's nearly time. It's struggling to contain the excitement, inching closer each time the beam sweeps across. The smell of fear is rife, and it sees it in them too, now. Air from its snout drifts over pipes jutting from its jaw, letting the others know that *it* will take the lead.

Fear oozes from his son's eyes, but Jack feels it, too. Impossible to rationalize, the music continues to increase in volume, and he swears he just saw a pair of yellow eyes puncture the darkness. He brushes his son's face, kisses his forehead, and finishes with the habitual ruffle. "We have to stay calm, okay? We'll be back at camp soon with a tale to tell." But his heart beats much faster than before.

Ethan nods, slaking his sleeve across his face, wisps of mist peppering the air around him. He sucks in a mouthful of damp air, trying to slow down his breathing, gain back some control. "Which way?"

Jack turns him back around and lifts his arm. "Straight ahead, champ. We've got this."

Ground cover claws at Ethan's feet as his weary legs carry him forward, the damned tune building to an ominous crescendo. There's a growing smell in the air too, above and beyond the mosses and wood and grass, something rotten that unsettles Ethan's stomach further. He makes it about fifty yards before paranoia overwhelms him, and he stops dead, snapping his head around and pointing the torch over his shoulder.

"Watch it, Eth!" his dad says, ducking out of the light.

Just trees, but he senses something out there among them. He turns fully, letting the light linger as if waiting for the yellow eyes to appear and for the terrifying growl of some godawful creature to signify imminent death. It's subtle, but the tune is changing. And again. And again. Ever so slightly on each loop, but it's undeniable. Chewing at his lip, he tries desperately to keep his arm steady, slowly sweeping the beam across the trees, unsure if it's paranoia or if the fucking things are moving. Not a wisp emerges from his mouth as the stand-off continues.

"Ethan, come on. Let's go!" Jack knows his voice comes out far from calm, but he's suddenly overwhelmed with the urgency to see another human.

"The ground, Dad." Ethan swallows hard, not a drop of saliva in his mouth. Both his hands are wrapped around the torch casing now. "It's moving!"

They both watch, mesmerized as the earth lifts, slowly and mechanically like a drawbridge, revealing guts of impossible darkness.

"Run," Jack croaks as the cloud emerges from the newly created crevice.

But Ethan is frozen to the spot, cheated by nature and rocked by the fear in his father's voice. The push on his shoulders, though, is enough to break the trance and he turns, instinctively beginning to run, the narrow beam dancing maniacally on the ground in front. Clouds of breath are displaced quicker than they form as Ethan pushes the pace, eyes searching the trees for anything familiar but mainly for those fucking yellow orbs or another patch of earth that might try and swallow them. He runs as fast as his legs can carry him, longing for the warmth of the fire and his mum's smile.

Trees and ground become a blur, and he visualizes the forest campaign on Call of Duty, pretending he's one of the brave soldiers leading the charge, the torch a gunsight for his AR-15, and the haunting soundtrack overlaid with explosions of mines, grenades, and the relentless spray of bullets. Undergrowth almost takes him down, but momentum saves him as he finds his feet and straightens up again, but he's sure as hell the shadows are moving. "This the right way, Dad?" He can no longer feel his legs, adrenaline almost floating him across the forest carpet. The sound of his footfalls raises awareness that the music has stopped, and relief sweeps over him, each new stride bringing feelings of imminent safety. They're going to make it. He glances over his shoulder to check on his father, and—all hope fades. He's nowhere to be seen.

Ethan slows himself to a halt and takes in mouthfuls of iciness, flashing the beam frantically into the trees. Moisture swells once again in eyes that already feel raw, but he refuses to let them escape, not right now. "Dad!" Blood pounding in his ears impossibly loud against the now deafening silence, he continues to light up the forest. Long spindly shadows reach toward him, and the trickle of moonlight only taunts. "Dad, where are you?" He cusses himself as a tear runs down his right cheek.

"Dad!"

The ground passes underneath, its harshness vibrating through Jack's spine. He can still see the dim light of the phone caught in tangled green. Ethan's desperate pleas continue to float across the forest, but all he can manage is a gurgled croak as the skinny and fleshy wet limbs snake around his chest. Futilely, he continues to claw at them but more appear, wrapping, constricting. He digs his heels into the mess and tries to call out, but the stickiness that drives farther into his throat steals his voice. He can taste the bitterness of rotting vegetation, but something else, something putrid. Fighting against the tendrils, he manages to turn his head, only to see the open pit waiting for him and the nothingness inside. He tries to call out again but finds himself plunged into darkness. Only as thickness finally leaves his throat does he manage a scream. "Run!" Winded, guilt gnawing at his insides, all he can do is watch the stars slowly begin to disappear as the lid comes down.

"Dad?"

The light of the torch carves an erratic path as Ethan spins around. Panic washes over him as all sense of direction fades. It's as if the forest is moving, ever-changing, trying to outfox. "Where are you?" Instinctively, Ethan wants to run, but he has no idea which direction will lead him to safety if there even is such a thing.

He catches a flash of yellow orbs ahead. To his right, more appear, but again, and just as quickly, they fade into black. Behind him, another two, burning brightly like embers but drifting into oblivion.

The first note drifts across the forest. And the second. Third. Fourth. Once again, the soundtrack is soon an unbroken symphony and closing in. Breathing fast and erratic but still not getting enough air, Ethan screws his face into the icy wind as it highlights the streams across both cheeks. *Which way? Which fucking way?* A whistle from behind spins him around—the bark of a tree—no, not bark at all; it's moving, pulsating—and the branches, twitching. Something else, too, the trunk is—

No! Fuck, no!

He's grateful that his legs carry him away from the jerking tree. His left arm pumping by his side, right arm rigidly extending the torch in front, his jog turns into a run, but the music only gets louder. He switches direction, praying this time that he's heading back to safety. His mind begins to race, but thoughts settle on the unopened packet of marshmallows on the back seat of the car and that he may never get to toast one over the orange flames.

Nothing looks familiar as he scans ahead. The truth is he wasn't really paying attention. His dad was by his side, making sure everything was going to be okay because that's what dads do. He fights the lump in his throat as he continues his sprint, knowing there's more than a chance he's moving farther away from the trail. "Help!" he cries.

This is the one *it* wanted. The others can have the older bitter flesh. Its snout twitches as it takes in the youngling's intoxicating secretions, and its stomach moans at the thought of such a feast. Usually, it takes what it can get:

rabbits, kangaroo, bird carcasses, but this will be a meal to be savoured. Excitedly, it extends its snout and releases air across the small pipes that jut out from its jaw.

Ethan listens intently over his heartbeat as he continues scrambling into darkness. He almost dares not to let himself believe, but it's definitely getting fainter, he's sure of it, and that can only mean—

It's just a slither of silver in the distance, but one that steals any remnant of hope. *No! No, please!* As he makes more ground, though, the stretched mouth and bulging eyes are unmistakable. "Dad, help me!" He bites at the inside of his cheek, the taste of metal forming quickly. Part of him wants to quit and find somewhere to hide and cower until the sun comes up, but the sight of the two yellow orbs to the left keeps him going. To his right, there are four more. At least a dozen behind. He aims the torch into the trees and kicks in, screaming as he runs past the stone faces. He doesn't see the void waiting for him, and as he finally slams against the ground and as blackness fills his vision, he expels a pained moan.

Excitedly, it makes its way across the forest floor, simultaneously snaking and using its tendrils to grab and pull it forward. It worries about others getting there first; it's happened before, and a fight to the death always ensues. The youngling is marked, though! *Its* plan! *Its* reward!

For a while, Ethan dares not to move and just lays there curled up in a crumpled heap, heavy earthiness laying at the back of this throat, mixed with that bad smell from before, only stronger. On the count of three, he grimaces and turns over, revealing the night sky framed by an almost perfectly square hole. Pain swells down his right side as he slowly begins dragging himself back toward the torch's thin beam, something sharp poking at his insides that doesn't feel right at all.

He stretches, teeth clenched, finally managing to grab the torch, but when he looks back up, two yellow orbs appear to be hovering above the rim. Resembling planets against the canvas behind, they quickly fall from the sky, and a heavy thud prompts Ethan to flick the beam ahead and scream until his voice is hoarse.

As white light basks the writhing grotesqueness that squirms toward him, Ethan continues to push back against the ground. His life quickly flashes before him, but thoughts turn once again to the unopened marshmallows on the back seat of the car. They were for tonight, a treat before heading home in the morning. Every thrust sends bolts of agony vibrating through his bones, but the thing continues to gain on him.

It's the wall of dirt that brings him to an undramatic halt. He tries to scream, but only a croak emerges. The twitching snout, the thick and slimy body that snakes toward him, eyes that reach into his soul, and the jutting pipes from the elongated jaw—even in nightmares, he's been unable to concoct such a beast, but this is nature's doing!

It writhes within only a few feet of him and stops, snout more active than ever, cutting and sniffing at the surrounding air. He lets out a whimper, desperately searching the wall for an opening, but his fingers only find more dirt. He knows it's over. The creature squirms a little closer, and he kicks out again, aware the display is less than pathetic. He follows its burning eyes, warmth spreading across his pants. He sees no teeth, no tongue, and the jaw—not a jaw at all, just an extension of the head.

It begins raising itself from the ground, glossy tendrils unwrapping from its body, and driving into the dirt until it stands as tall as a—tree. One of the shoots finds Ethan's left leg, another, his right. Helplessly, he watches the trunk—its body—begin to open, revealing a vertical mouth full of razor-sharp teeth and a marshy tongue that starts licking at the air.

As Ethan tries to drive himself through the wall, his hand brushes against something on the ground, and he glances down to see the patch of red tartan poking through the dusty covering. Cold sliminess wraps around his neck as he grabs the flask and brings it to his chest. Tears streaming, he smiles and holds it in the air. "I found it, Dad."

It drags the youngling toward its mouth.

THE END.

MARK TOWSE

Mark Towse is an Englishman living in Australia. He would sell his soul to the devil or anyone buying if it meant he could write full-time. Alas, he left it very late to begin this journey, penning his first story since primary school at the ripe old age of 45. Since then, he's been published in the likes of Flash Fiction Magazine, The Dread Machine, Cosmic Horror, Suspense Magazine, ParABnormal, Raconteur, and his work has also appeared on many exceptional podcasts such as The Grey Rooms, No Sleep, Creepy, Tales to Terrify, etc. His first collection, 'Face the Music,' was released by All Things That Matter Press and is available via Amazon, Dymocks, B&N, etc. His debut novella, 'Nana,' was published by D&T Publishing in March, also available via the usual outlets.

ROCK POOL OF THE GODS

DJ TYRER

A *staycation sucks*, thought Jenna as she sat, arms tightly folded, on a towel on a Cornish beach. All her friends—alright, most of her friends—were off to Spain or America or even to Brazil for the World Cup, but not only had her parents decided they didn't have the money for them to leave the country, but they'd somehow managed to choose the most distant, most boring village in Cornwall for their holiday.

The journey—first by train, then by taxi—had taken forever, and thanks to Dad's decision that phones and game consoles were incompatible with a family vacation, had been without any decent entertainment. Even her younger brother, Terry, was too old for I-spy and noughts-and-crosses, despite Dad's attempts to entertain them "the old-fashioned way." Mum just rolled her eyes and read her paperback.

Now they were in Penwarock, the situation was little improved. It had even rained the first day they were there. At least the sun—a wan sun, but a sun nonetheless—was out and she had the hope of a tan. Terry had spent a little time messing about in the sand but had soon lost interest.

"You kids should try wading in the rock pools," Mum said from behind her book. "There's all sorts of wildlife in the pools when the tide's out."

The tide was out, revealing a wide expanse dark rock undulating across the cove within which were numerous pools of saltwater left behind by the retreating tide.

"I s'pose," Terry grouched.

"You never know what weird and wonderful things we might discover," Dad added, standing up. "Come on."

Jenna and Terry followed reluctantly as he led the way, scrambling over slippery weed-festooned rocks and splashing through pools.

"See," Dad would say, pointing to something or other of interest: a seahorse or a starfish or an anemone. They had to admit it was actually kind of fun discovering what fascinating things called the pools home. Jenna had been to a SeaLife Centre on a school trip, but seeing the creatures close up like this in their home was quite different.

"Cool," said Terry, jabbing at an anemone with a fragment of driftwood to make it retract its fronds.

"Hey, don't hurt it," Jenna told him.

A moment later, as he splashed into the next pool, Terry let out a shriek of pain.

"My foot!" he shrieked, gesticulating wildly as Dad lifted him out of the water. Mum tossed her book aside onto the sand and came running to see what was wrong.

"Jellyfish," observed Jenna, pointing to the pool.

"Ouch," commented Mum as Terry sobbed in agony. His foot was a painful red where he'd been stung.

Dad reached for his trouser fly, saying, "I'll pee on it; that stops the pain."

"Eww!" exclaimed Jenna as Terry cried, "No fear!"

"Oh, put it away," ordered Mum. "We need to get him to the doctor to have the stingy-thingies removed and make sure there's no reaction or anything. Give me a hand; it's not far. The surgery's just a little way along from the guesthouse."

"I'll wait here," Jenna called after them. "Hey," she added, "if they chop his foot off, can I have his skateboard?"

"Don't be silly," Mum called back as Terry wailed at the thought of losing his foot.

"I'm just saying!" Jenna gave a cheerful wave as her parents supported her brother as he hopped up the beach and then the cobbled hill beyond. At least he'd managed to make things a bit more interesting. She laughed at his misfortune.

"Oh, well," she said to herself. "I might as well see what else there is..." and she continued along the rocks.

There was a peculiar shrimp in the next pool, shiny green with feelers twice the length of its body; it disappeared into a crack as she tried to get a closer look. As she pursued it, she thought she felt something brush past her leg. Glancing down, she saw what might have been a jellyfish.

Jenna gave a little shriek as she felt something soft and slimy squish beneath her foot. Scrambling quickly out of the pool, she looked down into the water but could see no sign of it. She felt no pain of a sting and gently tested her foot: nothing. She had to have been mistaken.

Deciding not to step back into the pool—just in case—she continued on her way, splashing through more pools until she heard Mum's voice calling to her. Looking back, she realized just how far from the shore she was.

"Jenna, the tide's on the turn," her mother called.

"Okay, Mum, I'm coming." She could see Terry was with them and appeared to still be in possession of both feet.

"Still alive?" she asked as she sat down beside him.

"Yeah, the doc removed the stings. It was nothing really."

Jenna managed not to laugh at that, remembering how he'd shrieked and hollered.

"Here you are," Mum said, handing her a towel.

Jenna began to towel herself off. As she did so, she realized she could feel something odd on the back of her heel, like an enormous blister. She laid the towel aside and probed it with her finger. Whatever it was felt soft and squishy beneath her finger and slightly slimy to the touch. With a start, she realized it must be the jellyfish-thing she'd trodden on in the rock pool: the thing had latched onto her heel like a leech! Could it be a leech?

"Eww, disgusting," she muttered, whipping her hand away.
She called Mum over.

"Mum, Mum, look at this, please."

"What is it, darling?"

"On my heel." She held her foot up and jabbed her finger toward it. "There's something on my heel—I think it's a leech—please, get it off!"

Her mother knelt and tilted her head to see. "Oh, Jenna, it's just a blister. That's all."

"No, Mum, I'm sure it's not: I was wading in one of the pools and I trod on something. I thought it was a jellyfish, but it didn't hurt—only now, it's stuck on me!"

Mum just laughed. "No, dear. It's just a blister, that's all. Put a plaster on it if it hurts."

"But Mum..."

"No buts, thank you. Get your shoes on, and we'll go have some fish and chips for supper."

That was another problem with Penwarock, the boring evenings and early nights. But right now, Jenna's mind was elsewhere.

"Come on, darling. Eat up," her Mum prompted as Jenna picked at her food. Jenna didn't really feel hungry; she wanted to get back up the hill so she could do something about the leech-thing. She felt a little sick to think of it attached to her like that. It was horrible.

Through the meal, barely eating, Jenna kept rubbing her heel against the leg of her chair, hoping to dislodge the thing. She could feel it squishing against the plastic, but it remained resolutely attached.

When finally they climbed back to the guest house, Jenna headed straight to the bathroom, grabbing one of Dad's blades for his razor on the way.

Sitting on the edge of the bath, her foot raised up, she could see the thing like a transparent jellyfish attached to her skin. Taking the razor, she tried to slice into it, but it just bulged out either side of the blade as she pushed it down. Then, gritting her teeth, she sliced into her skin, trying to cut it away.

Jenna clamped her free hand over her mouth to stifle her sobs and prevent herself from screaming at the pain. Blood ran freely, but she couldn't seem to detach the thing from her heel. Eventually, she gave up, dropped the blade into the bath, grabbed a wad of toilet paper, and pressed it against the cuts. Within moments, the paper was sodden and red with blood. She began to wonder if it would ever stop. But when she reached her fourth wad, it seemed to be slowing.

There was a first aid box on a shelf in the corner of the room, which she hopped over to and knocked to the floor with a crash.

"Jenna, you okay in there, love?" Mum called.

"Uh, yeah. I'll be out soon."

She found a plaster and stuck it over the cuts.

Maybe it *was* just a blister. Maybe she was just being silly. She tried to tell herself that, but she doubted it. But whatever it was, she couldn't get rid of it.

She gathered up the gory paper and flushed it, then rinsed her hands before washing the bath down. Finally, she wiped up any other spots of blood she could see until the bathroom seemed as pristine as it had been when she'd entered.

Throwing the blade into the bin, she put the first aid box back on the shelf. She winced a little as she put weight on her foot. She hobbled out the bathroom, stuck her head around her parents' door, and told them she was going to bed.

"Night, love," said Mum.

"G'night," called Dad with a yawn.

"Night," she replied. She called out "Night" as she passed her brother's room but could hear Terry was already snoring.

Reaching her room, Jenna climbed straight into bed. She still felt a bit nauseous and suddenly exhausted.

Within moments, she was asleep.

"Where am I?" Jenna asked, looking around in confusion. With a start, she realized that she was standing on the beach in Penwarock cove. Was she awake or was she dreaming?

Looking about, she could see that the beach was deserted, and she also realized there were no footsteps: she'd reached this place without leaving a single impression.

"It *has* to be a dream," she told herself. Yet it felt so real, more real than any dream she'd ever had: she could feel the coarse sand beneath her feet and smell the salt air.

"It has to be a dream," she repeated.

There was no moon in the sky, yet despite this, there was a glow illuminating the cover, a glow that appeared to emanate from one of the many rock pools far out along the undulating expanse of black rock. Something about the silvery-green light seemed to call her to it, irresistibly summoning her. She found herself walking toward it even without thinking.

After what seemed like too short a time, Jenna found herself standing beside the rock pool, half-blinded by the light that flowed up from the water.

Gazing down, she saw the shrimp—only of great size, as big as a grown man. The shrimp-thing was the source of the glow, emitting the silver-green light that flowed out almost like liquid. It appeared to gaze up at her with eyes like black pits that seemed to suck her into an infinite void.

Suddenly, Jenna felt herself falling, plunging down into the unnaturally deep pool of water, falling into the embrace of the shrimp-thing's long, flexing antennae. Her body felt strange: membranous was the term that somehow insinuated itself into her mind. She felt at one with the water about her and with the shrimp-thing that hugged her to it. She didn't need to breathe.

Jenna felt a strange sensation as she hung there gazing into those dark pit-like eyes, staring into infinity. She felt something divine and felt as if she were part of it.

Jenna woke with a start to the sound of knocking at her door and Mum calling her to breakfast. The sun flooded in through the window, harsh and golden, not at all like the light in her dream.

Instinctively, she slipped a hand beneath her covers and felt the back of her heel. The thing was gone! She threw back her covers and checked her bed: there were a few drips of blood from where her plaster had come away in the night, but no sign of the thing that had clung to her skin. She peeled the plaster away and could feel a scab, but the thing definitely had gone. A little paranoid, she checked her other foot, her legs, her arms, her body: no, it was definitely gone.

She gave a sigh of relief. Maybe it had only been a blister after all and had shrunk away as she slept.

There was only one slight, niggling problem: her foot did seem oddly numb, as if she had slept at an odd angle. Looking at it, her skin seemed pale.

"Could be because I cut it," she murmured to herself as she vainly attempted to massage life back into it, hoping that she hadn't done any damage.

"It'll be alright," she told herself before finally standing and dressing. She did find her gait awkward, her numb foot not quite supporting her, but she could walk well enough.

"You okay, love?" Mum asked when she joined them for breakfast. "You're limping."

"Oh, I'm okay. It's just that blister."

"Oh, dear. Did you put a plaster on it?"

Jenna nodded as she bit into some toast spread with rich Cornish butter.

"Well, if it causes you a problem, we could always take you to the doctor," Dad told her.

"Wuss," she heard Terry mutter.

"No, I'll be fine. I'm sure."

"Well, darling, do say if it gets worse," Mum said.

"I will," she told her, smiling somewhat weakly.

"Today," Dad said, "I thought we could take a trip up to the old ruins on the cliffs north of town."

"We can take a packed lunch," added Mum, "with proper Cornish pasties and a lovely cream tea. What do you say?"

"Whatever," muttered Terry but not too garrulously.

"Sounds good," Jenna assured them, thinking that getting away from the cove might do her some good.

But no matter what they did nor how far they walked, nothing could quite take her mind off the rock pool in her dream and the numbness in her foot which seemed to be spreading up her calf. Even the delicious packed lunch didn't interest her.

"Are you sure you're okay, love?" Mum asked. "You didn't eat much last night, and you're just pecking at your food now. You're not sickening, are you?"

Jenna shrugged. "I dunno. I don't feel quite right. My foot's gone kinda numb. You know, where I had that blister."

Mum was anxious, worrying that it could be flesh-eating bacteria or a deep-vein thrombosis, but Dad reassured her, saying, "It's probably just a tight shoe or something—it's given her a blister because it's too tight and now it's made her foot numb. Nothing to worry about. She'll be fine, you'll see—and if not, we'll take her to the doc tomorrow or up to A&E, have her looked at."

Mum nodded and Jenna agreed he was probably right.

"You'll live," Terry told her, patting his arm, but his tone sounded concerned, which surprised her, made her feel a little concerned.

By the time they walked back to Penwarock for a further meal of fish and chips, of which Jenna barely ate any, her entire leg seemed quite numb. Not that she said anything, hoping it would get better with time. Perhaps, she thought, a night's sleep would sort her out.

Jenna dreamt she was down in the cove again. If it was a dream. She felt detached from what was happening, yet something about it was more real than anything she'd ever experience before. Intense. *Supernatural.*

Once again, a glow was exuded by one of the pools to light the cove despite the lack of star or moonlight. A numinous silvery-green light that called her to it. Although she found herself walking across the undulating black rock, the motion was one of perception only; she couldn't feel anything physical.

It was as if she were a detached observer along for the ride, not the owner of her body; her body was no longer her own.

She reached the pool, the bright light streaming out, dazzling her vision.

"The Rock Pool of the Gods," Jenna heard herself saying, although she hadn't thought the words. Somehow, she knew the words were more than mere metaphor. The pool was sacred. Why and how she wasn't quite certain; she thought it was somehow related to the extrusion of volcanic rock from the bowels of the Earth, that it had brought something up with it, or perhaps something had descended here in flame from somewhere else. In her mind, there was a vision of fire and heat, the birth pangs of the divine: the divine that had touched her consumed her.

Jenna found herself falling down into the silvery-green waters, down into the embrace of the shrimp-thing's antennae. She felt as if she were merging into it. Her body was already one with it: would it subsume her mind as well?

Jenna woke feeling oddly numb. Her mind felt detached from her body as if it were floating a little way away from it. The sensation was similar to that in her dream: only more terrifying for being real.

She sat up and stumbled from the bed. Unlike in her dream, her movements were clumsy, not fluid, as if mind and body were not acting in concert.

Concentrating fiercely, Jenna forced herself to stumble to the bathroom where she stared in shock at her reflection in the mirror. It wasn't the peculiar, liquid sheen of her skin that disturbed her most, but the blister that covered one side of her face: a blister that seemed to pulse and quiver slightly. It was as if a jellyfish sat upon her cheek. Memories of fire and heat tugged at her mind: this was the stuff that had been borne into the rock pool by flame. This was what she was now.

Jenna wanted to scream, but although her lips twitched, no sound came out. She stumbled out of the bathroom and blundered into Mum's arms.

"Oh! What's that on your face!" Mum gasped.

Jenna tried to speak but couldn't. Her mind seemed to be drifting further away from her body, away toward oblivion.

Suddenly, the blister seemed to burst or propel from Jenna's face in a watery explosion to splash over Mum's. It covered her mouth and nose, and she collapsed, fingers clawing uselessly at it. Already it seemed to be flowing across her skin. Somehow, abstractly, Jenna knew that having absorbed her, the process of assimilation would be speedier for the others in her family. Shortly, Mum would also be subsumed into the divine.

Vaguely, Jenna wondered if she could kill herself to halt the theft of her body but knew it was already too late. What was left of her consciousness was fading away to nothing. Soon, her existence would be blotted out and what once had been her body would return to the waters of the rock pool to dissolve into a peculiar union with that which dwelt within it.

Eternally.

END

DJ TYRER

DJ Tyrer is the person behind Atlantean Publishing and has been widely published in anthologies and magazines around the world, such as Chilling Horror Short Stories (Flame Tree), All The Petty Myths (18th Wall), Steampunk Cthulhu (Chaosium), What Dwells Below (Sirens Call), The Horror Zine's Book of Ghost Stories (Hellbound Books), and EOM: Equal Opportunity Madness (Otter Libris), and issues of Sirens Call, Hypnos, Occult Detective Magazine, parABnormal, and Weirdbook, and in addition, has a novella available in paperback and on the Kindle, The Yellow House (Dunhams Manor).

DJ Tyrer's website is at https://djtyrer.blogspot.co.uk/

DJ Tyrer's Facebook page is at https://www.facebook.com/DJTyrerwriter/

The Atlantean Publishing website is at https://atlantean-publishing.wordpress.com/

TRIP TRAP

REBECCA ROWLAND

TRIP TRAP VACATION REVIEW

BAY BREEZE BEACH RESORT, CLEARWATER, FL

DENISE C.   **10 MONTHS AGO**

4/5 STARS

My husband and I stayed here for the first time last week. The place is huge! Seven floors, two restaurants, an indoor and outdoor pool, and three bars, not to mention a gigantic stage and dance floor right on the water. We were never at a loss for something to do, and we didn't even leave the premises. That being said, if you're looking for a hotel where you can hit the hay before sunrise and/or sleep through the night, make sure you request a street-facing room. The dance club opens at 10 p.m. and we could hear every bass thump from our fourth-floor room, even with the window closed and the a/c cranked. We'll likely return, but we'll be bringing ear plugs with us.

The overnight bag was small, but it was heavy, and the strap seemed to be digging deeper and deeper into Shannon's shoulder the longer they stood there. In contrast, as soon as they had hit the lobby, Lily had dumped her bag—a worn-out duffel leftover from her college days—onto the white tiled floor and simply slid it forward with her foot, soccer-pass style, as the line to check in crept along. At last, when it was their turn, Shannon blurted out her last name and handed over her credit card before the clerk's wooden smile could begin its practiced emergence from her lips. "And we'd like a room on the street side of the hotel, please," Shannon added.

Lily groaned. "Are you serious? We paid for a hotel on the beach. I'd like to see the *beach* from our bed."

Shannon's eyes did not move from the clerk's. "Street side," she repeated. "And as far up as possible, please." Only then did she turn to look at her girlfriend. "I researched this place thoroughly, okay? And I didn't bring my sleeping pills."

"We're on vacation," argued Lily. "Not at a sleep study." She raised her hands above her head and made a motion like she was pushing the ceiling. "Three days, two nights, and this is the first time we've been away in over a year."

"Okay, well, then, at least get two keys. In case I want to stay out later than you."

The clerk handed Shannon two key cards, still not smiling. "Room 713. Take a left off the elevator, and it's at the end of the hall on the right." She frowned at Lily. "Facing the street."

Shannon responded with a tight-lipped half smile, read-justed the torturing strap, and tucked the keys into a back pocket of her jeans. It was freezing in the lobby, and she was grateful she hadn't changed into shorts and a t-shirt at the airport as she first had planned.

The two women stood in the nearby hallway, staring word-lessly at the two elevator doors in front of them, the digital numbers above each gradually counting down. A sunburned college kid wearing aviator sunglasses and an old baseball shirt joined them. The man leaned forward as if the two women's refusal to acknowledge him was simply due to his being out of range of their vision.

"Hey, girls," he said. "You just get here? My name's Tom." He thrust his hand in front of Shannon's breasts, stopping only an inch from her sweatshirt zipper. Men were always ogling Shannon, and she had learned to ignore the flickering gazes, but it still irked Lily at times, even after three years of living together.

Lily turned and positioned herself in front of Tom, then grabbed his hand and shook it hard. "Hi there, Tim. I'm Daisy, and this here little lady is my sister Mae. We sure do appreciate the welcome wagon!" Her voice had taken on an exaggerated drawl Shannon only heard when Lily was talking down to someone.

Tom backed away a step. "Uh, it's *Tom*, actually. You're sisters, huh?" He paused, thinking for a moment, then a mischievous grin angled up across one side of his face. "Vacationing together? Gonna let loose and have some fun?"

Lily let go of Tom's hand and instead stepped back and wrapped her arm around Shannon, bringing their faces so close together, Shannon could smell the Chapstick on her lips. "Nothing gets by you, Tim," Lily said. Then, in a move she often did when she wanted strangers to keep their distance, she stuck out her tongue and ran it from the bottom of Shannon's cheek to her temple, maintaining eye contact with Tom the entire time.

Tom's face raced through expressions like a deck of cards in the middle of a dealer's shuffle and finally resigned itself to one of confused repulsion. He turned to face the still-closed elevator doors and muttered under his breath.

"What was that, Tim?" Lily cocked her hand around her ear like she was listening for a far-away alarm bell. The silvery doors on the left slid open, and the car emptied quickly, but Tom turned on his heel and walked quickly toward the door on the opposite end of the foyer marked Stairway. Lily snatched her bag from the floor, and the two women got onto the elevator alone.

"You don't have to be so hostile all the time, you know," Shannon said, pushing the button marked 7. "He's just some stupid frat boy. There are a million down here. The South and Mid-West states might as well abbreviate themselves with Greek letters."

Lily rolled her eyes. "How sad is that? Poor Southern and Midwesterners: they have to make people in their college swear an oath to promise to be their friends forever. Like when you're a kid and your parents make you play with their friends' kids, and you have to be nice to them or else. So pathetic."

The car rose one floor and stopped. When the doors opened, a small cleaning woman pushing a laundry cart wheeled into the car. Without acknowledging the women, she reached across and pressed 3. As she did, the sleeve on her right arm pushed up toward her elbow, and Shannon couldn't help but stare. Her olive skin was covered in large red welts, raised blisters with pinprick dots in the centers like tremendous bug bites.

The woman caught Shannon's gaze and quickly pulled her cuff down to her wrist and tucked her hands behind the cart. Oblivious to the exchange, Lily turned to face the woman. "Ma'am, do you know if there are Coke machines on the floors?" She ran her fingers through her hair and glanced at Shannon. "I'm super thirsty. We should've gotten something when we landed."

The elevator dinged, and when the doors opened, the woman wordlessly pushed her cart forward, turned left, and disappeared out of sight. Lily and Shannon looked at each other and couldn't help but laugh. "Staff is super helpful here, I guess?" Lily said. "Chatty."

Shannon patted her on the shoulder softly, a move she found herself doing more and more often, like her mother did to her father. "How about we dump this stuff in the room, get changed, and go down to the pool bar?"

Lily once again wrapped her arm around her girlfriend, but this time, she pulled Shannon's head closer to hers and kissed her playfully on the forehead. "Now you're talking, sister."

Trip Trap Vacation Review

Bay Breeze Beach Resort, Clearwater, FL

Reina L.   7 months ago

1/5 stars

Enjoyed the food, the pool (bar area with Todd) and even the club, but the room was so f***ing gross. (See photo) Yes, that is a pair of someone's UNDERWEAR hanging from the shower wall. We called the front desk to get a new room, but they said they were booked and offered to re-clean it, but the lazy ass maid only removed the panties. She didn't wipe up the bristles of hair that were all over the tub. I mean, they were ten times nastier than regular stranger hair: thick and black, and like an inch long—did someone shampoo their pet boar in there?? Anyways, the only silver lining was that we scored a room facing the street so we didn't have to hear the constant beach noise like everyone seems to be complaining about on here. Boyfriend still had the TV blaring all night. He claimed could hear the people next door "rustling" around in their beds. I don't know. I slept okay. I didn't shower all weekend, though.

It was after four o'clock, and the beach had gotten progressively busier as the day wore on. Shannon was glad Lily had rented chaises for them, but she had been drinking vodka and grapefruit juice like water, or more accurately, instead of water, and she was starting to feel a bit loopy. It didn't help that they'd forgone renting an umbrella in the hope that they could infuse a week's worth of tan from just two days of prolonged sunbathing, but Shannon's skin was beginning to feel like a fallen apple after it's been left outside to blister in the sun for days. She sat up and patted her hand beneath the chair to feel for her shirt.

Lily turned her head and lifted her sunglasses. "Where are you going?"

"It's too hot," Shannon said. "I gotta cool off for a bit."

Lily sat up. "Want to go swimming?" As she said it, a pair of jetskiiers slid onto the edge of the shore, spraying a rush of water onto some nearby pre-teens playing in the sand. The children began to scream as if on fire.

"Nah," said Shannon, pulling the shirt down over her bikini top. "I just need to get out of the sun for a while. Plus, I have to pee. Need anything?"

Lily twisted her body around and relaxed onto her stomach. "Pee for me too," she said in a sleepy voice.

Shannon stepped into her shorts and then her flip-flops. She felt for the room key in her back pocket, just in case she wanted to buy something at the bar after all, and walked as gracefully as she could in the dense white sand past the hotel's outside pool.

She pushed her sunglasses onto the top of her head and opened the glass door to the hotel lobby. A cold gasp of air slid past her and escaped into the world. There were two restrooms just inside to the left, and Shannon ducked into the one marked "Ladies," catching her pink reflection in the mirror immediately inside. The lights weren't on, but there was plenty of natural light streaming in from the windows sidling the ceiling. The temperature was at least forty degrees cooler inside, but instead of feeling relief, her skin seemed to shrivel at the sudden drop. No one else was in the bathroom, so she chose the first stall out of convenience, wrestled her shorts and bathing suit bottom down to her knees, and sat on the toilet.

The stream of urine felt hot as she released it. She poked her finger at the skin on her right thigh, watching the place where she pressed turn white then fill with color again. She'd either have a decent base tan by the evening or a wicked burn: she couldn't tell. Her head still felt foggy, and she propped her chin in her fist and leaned forward, her elbow on her knee, and closed her eyes. When she opened them again, her head was facing the floor, and that was when she saw the bug.

No—bug was the wrong word for it. It could only be called a beetle. Or a *roach*. It was nearly two inches long; its body and spindly legs a deep, shiny black. Thin antennae wiggled at its head as it seemed to be considering Shannon's bright yellow flip-flop from a half foot away.

Palmetto bug, Shannon thought. She'd heard of these disgusting things from her aunt, who often vacationed in the Carolinas and had discovered one or two in the cabins where she'd stayed. *Christ, they're enormous.*

It's more afraid of you than you are of it. This bizarre piece of advice, something she could not attribute to any one person but had definitely heard in more than one context, echoed in her head. *Keep your eye on it*, her mind responded. *The only thing that's worse about seeing a creepy bug is not knowing where it goes.*

In one fell swoop, she yanked her suit and shorts back up to her hips and stood up. She stomped her foot hard on the tile floor, expecting the roach to scurry off somewhere into the dark recesses of the hotel bar's plumbing. Instead, the bug bolted forward and made a beeline toward Shannon. For a moment, Shannon thought of the raccoons she saw in her backyard each summer. *If they don't run away from you, they're probably rabid*, Lily would say, *so just keep away from them.*

Shannon pushed the stall door open and ran for the exit, not bothering to flush, wash her hands, or even button her shorts.

TRIP TRAP VACATION REVIEW

BAY BREEZE BEACH RESORT, CLEARWATER, FL

JAKE B.   5 MONTHS AGO

5/5 STARS

Writing this as we chill in the Tampa airport on our way home to Philly. Me and my boys had a *kickin* bachelor party for my man Steve at the Bay Breeze! We got stuck with a boring ass room way up on the

*top floor with nothing to see on our side but the
Sunoco and some pirate mini golf place across the
street, but it's all *obama* cause we hooked up with
some fresh girls with a room overlooking the dance
floor. Only thing that sucked is someone must of
brought a ferret or something. My duffel bag got golf
ball sized holes all over the side with tiny teeth marks
like something chewed on it all weekend.*

"Want me to get you something and bring it up to the room?"
Lily sat on the edge of the bed and stroked Shannon's hair.
"You hardly ate any dinner."

Her girlfriend was lying on top of the quilt. Shannon's face
and chest were a deep ferocious red; even her lips looked
puffy and sore. "It's okay," she answered. "I took a few Tylenol
and drank a ton of water. I just want to nap for an hour. You
go on down." Lily raised her eyebrow and looked dubious, but
Shannon patted her hand. "I'll text you when I'm on my way.
Really. Go."

Lily stood up. "Okay. I'll go down and scope out stuff while
you're napping, and then we can decide what we want to do."

"Do me a favor and shut off the air conditioner before you
go? Maybe open the window? It's freezing in here."

Lily complied, the wall unit shuttering to a wheezy stop,
then sighing. The windows were the ancient, hand-crank style,
and they hadn't been opened in quite some time, so it took
a bit of wrestling, but finally, the smells of salt and sand tem-
pered with car exhaust drifted into the room.

Shannon turned painfully onto her side and looked at the
window. "It's so nice to see the sun and blue sky," she said.

Lily laughed. "We live in Massachusetts, not in a bunker.
We have sun and sky."

"No...the air smells different here, you know?" said Shannon,
closing her eyes. "The sun is different here, everything feels
different. Softer. Like the whole state has been tumbling in a
dryer with one of those anti-static sheets."

"Yeah, I don't know about the anti-static thing. You should
have seen the hair on this chick that walked by me after you

went to the bathroom," quipped Lily. "A walking Poison reunion poster." When she looked at Shannon again, she was asleep.

The slight murmur from the traffic and street activity had died down by the time Shannon woke up. The light outside was dim, but it wasn't quite fully dark. At first, she was confused; she patted the space on the bed beside her, and the quilt was cool and empty. But then, as she sat up, the hot pulsing of her sunburn reminded her where she was, and she leaned over to turn on the light on the nightstand. Far below the window, somewhere on the street, a gaggle of people were laughing. Someone drinking too much, too early in the day. She couldn't throw stones.

As the group moved on down the street, their noise softened, and it was then that Shannon heard the other noise. A rustling, like leaves... and yet, not leaves exactly, but more like a thousand needles scratching against dry paper. She sat as still as she could, trying to pinpoint from where the sound was coming. It sounded like the headboard, but when she pressed her ear against the plain wood, she knew that wasn't the place, but it was close.

Shannon stood up next to the bed and faced it. The scratching was coming from the wall behind the headboard. And not from one area of the wall, but from the whole wall. Something within the wall, behind the wall, was scratching, tunneling, chewing; hissing and tearing at the air like a big white noise machine.

She walked over to the wall and pressed her cheek against the faded, antiquated wallpaper. Something was behind the wall, or maybe just behind the wallpaper. As she pressed her cheek harder, she thought she felt the wall shift and press back, an undulating wave like a rolling massage mat, gliding its tongue along the side of her face.

TRIP TRAP VACATION REVIEW

BAY BREEZE BEACH RESORT, CLEARWATER, FL

JANna O.   3 MONTHS AGO
                        5/5 STARS

OMG my husband and I had such a great time at the Bay Breeze!! He's not really a beach person, so we drove into the city during the day, and we found this AMAZING popsicle place that sells these things called Hyppo Pops, which were so delicious I actually cried a little when I finished my blackberry goat cheese one. At night, we went to the Iguana Bar next door to the hotel, and it's a hopping tiki-bar where you can sip Pina Coladas right on the beach! We went back to the Bay Breeze after and sat at the bar nearest to the hotel (my husband doesn't like loud noise) and met other couples there who were super nice! My husband says they were swingers and had been trying to get with us for the night, but I think he's just being silly. I took lots of pictures but Trip Trap only lets you upload ten so here are all the best ones.

The Iguana was packed with people, but it wasn't anything Shannon and Lily found unusual. They were still in their twenties when bar-hopping and or a Tool concert were completely worth it even when they couldn't hear or eat solid food the following day. Lily had explored the block while Shannon was asleep, and in addition to buying an obscene amount of ibuprofen ("to help your sunburn, and also, in the likely event I have a wicked hangover tomorrow morning"), she found the tiki-bar attached to the hotel next door to the Bay Breeze Resort. "It's supposed to have a ton of great pub food," Lily said. "Plus, it's right on the beach."

They had eaten dinner, a large meal in comparison to what they usually ate, but somehow, Lily was slurring her words at eleven o'clock at night. "Why can't I dance? I don't understand,

Shanannarama." It was her pet name, the one she took out and presented as an offering when she really wanted something Shannon was hesitant to give.

"I think we can all agree, despite alcohol consumption, that uncoordinated twerking is never something friends let friends do: not in public or in private, my love," Shannon replied, grasping Lily's face in her hands and kissing her long and hard.

Lily pulled away and smiled. "But I like dancing." Her voice cartwheeled and somersaulted in the air.

"Didn't you say you had to use the ladies' room?" Shannon didn't mind when Lily drank too much. Although they scrubbed the bathroom weekly without exception, the unspoken rule was whoever throws up in the toilet that week cleans it. And Lily was a happy drunk, at least. She hoped it would always be this way.

When Lily departed, Shannon continued to sip her drink and gaze about the room. Across the bar, a fidgety man wearing a coral-colored tank top two sizes too big was chatting up a petite woman by his side. She was likely his wife, Shannon thought; they both had that lived-in look to them. As he spoke, more into the woman's hair than into her ear, he kept readjusting the shirt, pulling it forward so that it nearly exposed a nipple. Finally, he reached a hairy arm over his shoulder and scratched the top of his back. The woman remained uninterested, concentrating her attention on a television set hanging from the ceiling. Big Tank stopped talking and began to scan the room with his eyes, his hand continuing to pick and burrow into hidden skin.

A gust of Gulf breeze stroked Shannon's back and tousled her hair. She was beginning to move her gaze onto another patron when Big Tank turned his body to face the tables behind him, giving Shannon a clear view of his back. The billowy shirt had fallen backward, revealing the flesh on his upper shoulders. As he pulled his hand away, it was finally clear what had been causing his insatiable itch: the tanned, hairless skin was covered in bulbous welts at least an inch wide, pustules with tiny pinpricks exactly like the ones on the arm of the woman on the elevator. These eruptions, however, were crisscrossed with deep red lines where the man's fingernails had dug at the irritation. She watched in horror as the man reached another hand to his back, raking it furiously until one of the pustules tore open, and deep red blood began to pool at the break.

Shannon nearly knocked Lily down as she ran headfirst into her on her flight out of The Iguana and into the street.

TRIP TRAP VACATION REVIEW

BAY BREEZE BEACH RESORT, CLEARWATER, FL

LIZ G.   1 MONTH AGO

3/5 STARS

We usually stay in Key West, but this year, with the hurricane damage, we had to find a new place to go, so we looked at places on the Gulf Coast. Unfortunately, this resort just did not meet our expectations. The beach was super crowded during the day with jet skiers always blocking access to the water. The breakfast was nothing special, neither great nor awful, and the hotel room itself was clean but really old. The wallpaper looked kind of scratched up, and it was torn in a few places, and there was a big, dark brown stain on the carpet next to the bed. When we went to get ice from the bin at the end of the hall, we spotted a hole in the wall next to the cooler: a big hole, like someone had put a fist through it, and a few more dark brown stains around the edges.

Lily was drooling on her as they kissed, something that wasn't on its own a deal-breaker, but combined with her inability to shake the image of Big Tank's back, she knew her head was nowhere near where it should be for good sex. She pushed Lily off of her and sat up.

"What's wrong?" her girlfriend asked, at a volume about two clicks too loud for a bustling nightclub, never mind a hotel at three in the morning.

"Shhh," Shannon whispered. "You're screaming."

Lily rolled onto her back and put her hands behind her head. "What? Are you afraid the neighbors will hear me? I doubt anyone's even next door. We haven't heard a peep, not even a toilet flush or a television."

Shannon was quiet for a minute, and then: "Have you ever seen a bed bug?" She glanced about the room, wondering what the signs of an infestation were.

Lily thought for a moment. "No, I haven't. They're supposed to be pretty nasty, though. Why? Do you have a rash or something? The man you saw in the bar: that's really bothering you?"

"No... I—" Shannon ran her hands along the bed sheets. They were stiff, but the subtle pilling reminded her of how many other people had pressed their skin against them. She eyed her overnight bag on the floor of the open closet and thought of the cleaning woman's arm, of the man in the bar's back. Should she move the bag to the top of the dresser? Could bed bugs crawl up walls? "I just think that—" she began to finish her thought, but when she turned to face Lily again, she could see her girlfriend had passed out cold.

Instead, she looked at the bed sheet. She imagined a million tiny beetles crawling inside of the mattress below her, burrowing through the stuffing and filling the springs. She got up from the bed and walked to the window. Lily had closed it when they returned home and had turned the air conditioner on low, but Shannon was cold again, so she shut it off.

Lily began to snore. Her mouth gaped open, and Shannon imagined the big Palmetto bug, the one from the bathroom, crawling inside of it.

The air conditioning unit powered down slowly. The final fan whirred and rattled, then fell mute. There was a beat of complete silence, and then... the scratching in the wall began. It was the same sound Shannon had heard earlier, but this time, it seemed louder, amplified like Lily's voice became when it was soaked in alcohol.

The scratching, like a million tiny needles, was everywhere in the wall, a collective consciousness of sound, and she placed her hand on the area of the wall closest to her and felt the movement below: a million tiny fingers ticking and tapping a Morse code softly into her palm.

Shannon scanned the wall; she could see where the strips of wallpaper met: it was right behind the bed, a foot or so behind Lily's head. She climbed back onto the bed, then stood upright in front of her pillow and reached her hand to touch the seam. If she held her hand *just so*, she thought she could feel it: something was pushing against the seam, trying to break the seal. She looked toward the ceiling and spotted a small section where the old glue had finally given up, an edge that had broken free of the wall and was jutting slightly away. If she stretched her arm, really reached, she could touch it, and she did. Perhaps if she could pull the paper away, she could see what was hiding beneath it.

Shannon shifted onto her tip-toes but only managed to sink farther into the mattress. She moved closer to Lily's snoring face and stepped on the pillow. Stretching her arm and lengthening her body as far as she could, she finally grasped the errant flap in between her thumb and fingers and pulled, but as she did so, she lost her balance and tumbled backward onto the mattress, the edge of wallpaper still clutched in her fist.

The piece that ripped from the wall was about the size of Shannon's hand, but it revealed something extraordinary. The naked plaster was, indeed, moving, but it wasn't a wave looping over and over, as she had imagined. Just beneath the wall's skin was a bump slightly smaller than the size of her fist, running wildly back and forth. Was it another one of those Palmetto bugs? She shivered instinctively at the thought.

Shannon snatched one of her flip-flops. Without thinking, she began to slap the exposed plaster with it, but the action was woefully ineffective. The movement continued, unfettered. She dropped the shoe and glanced quickly around the room for something more substantial. There was a small iron, *for our guests' convenience*, sitting at the top of the closet. As fast as she could, Shannon leaped from the bed and retrieved it. She'd quiet the scratching, and then she and Lily could get a good night's sleep and relax the rest of the weekend. It was okay if a few bangs woke up her girlfriend: neither of them could be expected to sleep with a giant beetle running back and forth behind their heads, could they?

She smashed the iron against the lump, but each time, the movement continued; the scratching, in fact, seemed to grow louder. Shannon struck the plaster over and over, a twisted game of Whack-a-mole gone horribly wrong.

Lily opened her eyes and looked around, confused. As she began to lift her head and sit up, the edge of the iron's metal plate hit the plaster just right and broke the surface. The wall stopped undulating, and the rustling abruptly silenced, like the breaking of a neck at the end of a hangman's noose.

Shannon walked awkwardly but triumphantly backward on the bed, trying to maintain her balance, and smiled at Lily. Her girlfriend looked in horror at the baseball-sided hole Shannon had made. Neither of them said anything for a long minute, and then, the wall spilled its secret. A waterfall of black exoskeletons and legs and antennae erupted from the maw, spraying Lily's face with clicking, ticking roaches. The whole wall rippled, pushing its contents through the hole like a terrible birth, and Shannon dropped the iron squarely on her bare foot.

Trip Trap Vacation Review

Bay Breeze Beach Resort, Clearwater, FL

Jeannie M.   1 week ago

4/5 stars

Fun in the sun! Great drinks! Great location! Staff is kind of blah, though. I went to the front desk to ask for a band-aid, and the concierge just stared at me, saying nothing. Whatever! Cool water sports, and a fun dance floor right on the beach with a HUGE screen that displays light shows and video. Bring a sweatshirt for sure. They keep the lobby and restaurants super cold; everyone who worked there seemed to be wearing long pants and long sleeves like we were in Alaska in the winter or something. Also, we'll probably explore other places to eat when we return next break. We got a huge plate of nachos in the restaurant, and I think they left our plate under the heat lamp too long ,'cause everything, even the black olives—and there were like, a million of them—were crunchy. Otherwise, totally awesome time!

REBECCA ROWLAND

Rebecca Rowland is an Active member of HWA and the dark fiction author of the short story collection The Horrors Hiding in Plain Sight, co-author of the novel Pieces, and curator of the horror anthologies Ghosts, Goblins, Murder, and Madness; Shadowy Natures, The Half That You See, and Unburied: A Collection of Queer Dark Fiction. For links to the cutting-edge publications where her work has appeared most recently, or just to surreptitiously stalk her, visit RowlandBooks.com.

ERUPT

EVAN BAUGHFMAN

The ATV rumbled beneath Esther as she climbed the rain-forest trail. She was careful not to twist the throttle too hard. A sudden burst of speed would plow her straight into Brendan's ride. Yes, they'd had their share of arguments lately, but Esther didn't have any real desire to see her twin brother somersault down a mountainside.

Plus, at their current pace, Esther was able to appreciate the view. The trail snaked through a kaleidoscope of different greenery: massive ferns and towering trees. Blue butterflies frolicked between frequent flower bursts. Above, the sun shone through gaps in the leafy canopy. Surely, cheery birds chirped, but ATV engines and a thick safety helmet dulled Esther's ability to hear nature's song.

At this elevation, the air was crisp and cool, too, and not at all how Esther had imagined South American weather to be. She was thankful to be wearing a sweatshirt and jeans. Brendan, on the other hand, once again wore shorts and a red fútbol jersey, his costume for their entire stay in Chile.

The back of his jersey said "SÁNCHEZ," the moniker of some popular player on the national team. For the past year or so, Brendan had fallen in love with their Chilean heritage, even though he'd barely managed to get a "D" in Spanish II. He and Esther were California kids, more familiar with In-N-Out cheeseburgers than malaya, no matter how much Brendan denied it to be true.

The jersey seemed to have earned him some new friends, however, including their trail guide, Mateo, a goateed man with a ponytail who, by Esther's approximations, was about thirty years old. Mateo's age, though, hadn't prevented him from leering at Esther, an almost-junior in high school.

Mateo rode up ahead of Brendan. He'd given the twins a twenty-minute ATV tutorial before deeming them trail-ready.

Behind Esther was another ATV, this one driven by Dr. Gabriel Castillo, though the doctor preferred to be called "Dad."

Their father was a renowned geologist who specialized in volcanoes—their structure and their activity. Back home, Brendan told people that Dad was a "volcanologist," while Esther preferred not to mention him at all.

When Esther and Brendan were in kindergarten, Dad had left the family to "chase lava" as Mom had put it. He wrote letters and made birthday phone calls for a while, but eventually that was all swallowed up by lava, too.

Fifteen months ago, Dad reconnected with his children. He said he lived in Chile now, his birth country, and wouldn't it be fun someday if Brendan and Esther chose to visit him there for summer vacation?

Brendan was ecstatic for the opportunity. He read everything he could find about the place, often bragging that he knew the differences between alpacas, guanacos, and vicuñas.

Esther, on the other hand, was less than thrilled about spending weeks abroad with a stranger who, for a decade, had chosen magma over her.

Now, though, Esther realized there were worse ways to spend July. Fireworks couldn't hold a Roman candle to ascending a volcano atop an ATV.

And she had to admit: Chile was beautiful, far more picturesque than her smoggy part of the world. After picking his kids up from the airport, Dad had driven them through an everlasting landscape of mountain ranges, lakes, and vegetation.

"There are two thousand volcanoes in this country," Dad had explained. "Most of them are dormant and covered in trees. Volcanic soil's packed with nutrients. Supports all kinds of life. Lots of mythology about these mountains, but it literally all boils down to simple science."

"That's why you're here," Brendan had said. "The volcanoes."

"Not many of those back home," Esther had added. "Just us, your kids."

"Damn, Esther. Ease up."

Dad's reply: "I tried America for as long as I could, but Chile has always been my home. It has a better sense of community. Kind, loving, spiritual people. A few bad apples here and there, sure, but far less rotten at its core than the United States is, let me tell you.

"For years, I tried convincing your mother that we could move here as a family. Actually get to know and love our neighbors. She didn't like that idea, though. She prefers the city life.

"I'm sorry, but it ate away at me for a long, long time. So, eventually, I had to make a decision."

"You left."

"That's right, Esther. I left. It was a tough decision. And it took me too long to realize it was the wrong one. Okay? From this day forward, I'm going to make things up to you. I promise, this is a new beginning for the Castillo family. You'll see."

Currently, on the ATV, all Esther wanted to see was a pudú, the world's smallest—and cutest!—deer. Her eyes searched rainforest foliage for the creature. Brendan had mentioned wanting to see a pudú, too, but only if it were eviscerated and hanging inside a puma's jaws.

The teens would take photos of it with their phones either way.

Up ahead, Mateo raised a hand, signaling the party to stop. Caught off-guard, Esther accidentally revved the throttle for a moment instead of pulling the hand brake.

She bumped into Brendan's ATV. He turned around in his seat and generously gifted his sister a middle finger. Esther returned in kind.

Fifty meters away, a small pick-up truck blocked the trail. Standing in front of the truck were two men. Each held a rifle.

Mateo turned back to the family and shouted in English, "Don't worry. I think I know them. Amigos, from the village." He then turned off his engine and walked toward the men, his helmet in hand.

"Dad?" said Brendan, beginning to remove his helmet, too. "What's going on?"

The doctor pointed to his son's headgear. "Hey, don't take that off." Then, to both of his children: "Keep your engines running."

They had to practically yell to hear one another.

Earlier in the day, Dad had described Mateo as a "good acquaintance," someone he'd drunk beers with a time or two. A week ago, when Dad had mentioned that his kids were coming for a visit, Mateo had offered the ATV experience.

Dad's original plan was to take Esther and Brendan up the volcano anyway, but inside his rickety Jeep. He figured, though, that an ATV adventure would probably be more fun.

Esther had agreed with that sentiment. Until now.

Although, it seemed like Mateo knew the gun-toting men at the truck, after all. The amigos laughed about something, glanced back at the Castillo trio, and grinned.

Mateo's thumbs-up gesture to the family didn't do much to assuage the anxiety building inside Esther's chest, however. Dad didn't seem to be feeling too comfortable, either.

The men weren't putting their guns aside. In fact, one of them secured his rifle stock against his shoulder and practiced peering down the sight. The weapon's barrel was, thankfully, aimed at the ground.

Brendan had his phone out, recording the scene. Dad suggested the armed duo might not appreciate being filmed. Brendan pocketed the device.

Behind his sunglasses, Dad's eyes studied the roadblock. He said, "Get ready to go, you two."

"Go where?" Brendan asked. "They're in the way."

"Back," said Dad. "Down the mountain."

Brendan was annoyed. "Why? We just barely started, like thirty minutes ago." His "pal," Mateo, had promised them a three-hour tour.

"There might be trouble," Dad explained.

Esther gulped. "What kind of 'trouble'?"

"This volcano, *Cerro Verde*...For many of the locals, it's sacred. Thought I was working here long enough to have gained some trust, but maybe not everyone's happy to have more than one American poking around."

"We're Chilean, though." Brendan shouted to the men at the truck, "*¡Somos chilenos!*" Google Translate had taught him the phrase two days ago.

Esther urged her brother to "Shut up!"

Brendan glared at her. "You, shut up!"

Esther now saw one of the men talking on a cell phone while the other joked with Mateo, clapping him on the back.

"Dad," said Esther, "I want to go."

"So do I," said Brendan. "Farther up the trail."

Dad replied, "Probably not today, bud."

"Why not? What do they even think we're going to do to this place?"

Dad shrugged. "I'll try to find out, once we're back in town."

Brendan pouted. "This sucks." He yelled, "Hey, Mateo, what's the verdict, huh?"

Mateo held up a finger, signaling for them to wait. "*¡Uno momento!*"

"Dude, if we have to go back already, I'm going to be pissed."

Esther said, "I'll live with whatever the guys with the guns want us to do."

"I don't get it," said Brendan. "They think we're going to kidnap a condor or something?"

Dad shrugged. He called out, "*¡No queremos problemas, Mateo! ¿Podemos ir, por favor?*"

Mateo consulted the other men, who nodded. He replied, "First, Gabriel, come here. Yeah? For a little conversation."

Those blue butterflies had somehow fluttered their way inside Esther's stomach. "Dad, don't."

"Stop," said Brendan. "Maybe he can convince them to let us pass."

Esther looked to her brother. "Are you high?"

"You know, I really wish you hadn't packed your pessimism for this trip."

Dad turned a key, silencing his ATV. He stood in the middle of the trail and said to the kids, "Your engines stay running. Don't be afraid to leave me behind if you have to."

Esther and Brendan watched their father approach the truck.

Brendan asked, "Why the hell would we leave him behind?"

One of Mateo's friends raised his rifle and shot Dad right in the chest.

A cacophony of multi-colored birds exploded from their treetop roosts, disappearing farther into the forest. Esther shrieked along with them. Brendan stared, speechless, at their father lying motionless on the ground.

After Esther saw Mateo high-five the shooter, she screamed, "Go, Brendan! GoGoGO!!!"

He snapped out of his daze and said, "Oh, shit!" as the men started moving their way.

Brendan turned the throttle and steered his ATV in a wide arc around Dad's body. Esther tried to do the same, but she gunned her throttle. The vehicle nearly leapt out from under her like a wild animal.

Still, she was able to corral the beast and manage a U-turn like her brother had. As she moved past Dad, Esther thought she saw him breathing.

Please, God! Please!

She slowed her ride. She could lift him onto the back of her ATV somehow...No, he was too heavy. Twice her size!

"Come on. COME ON!" Brendan was yelling at Esther now.

Behind them, the men approached, crying, "¡Alto, alto!"

Screw that!

"We have to leave him!" said Brendan. "Like he said!"

"Oh, God! Dad, I'm..."

SorrySorrySORRY!!!

Esther banked the guilt for later, and the twins zoomed down Cerro Verde with Brendan in the lead.

Esther remembered dips and rocky patches in the trail, but she couldn't quite remember where they had been. And ATVs—of course!—didn't come with seatbelts.

"Be careful, Brendan!"

But he probably didn't hear her over his adrenaline, his engine.

Wind pelted Esther's face, stinging her cheeks pink. Bugs ricocheted off her gritted teeth.

What are we going to do?

WhatWhatWhat???

Get the police.

YeahYeahYeah!!!

PolicePolicePolice!!!

Ahead of them, another truck appeared, scaling up the trail.

Thank God!

ThankyouThankyouThankyou!!!

Esther slowed her descent and starting waving a hand to get the driver's attention. "*¡Ayuda!*" she screeched. "*¡Ayúdanos!*"

But then she saw a man rise up in the truck's bed. Against the truck's roof, he positioned a rifle in the kids' direction.

Oh, God.

NoNoNo!!!

"Brendan!"

He wasn't slowing down. He wasn't going to stop.

Not for a truck. Not for a gun.

He was going to try to maneuver around this new batch of locals: the rifleman and two others in the cab.

"Brendan, don't!"

The truck sped toward him. Brendan increased his own downward velocity.

"BRENDAN!"

The rifle fired, twice. The second bullet struck one of Brendan's front tires.

The ATV rolled, flinging the boy over its handlebars, momentarily crushing his legs before disappearing into a tangle of bushes.

Brendan twisted on the ground in agony. His phone had been thrown from his pocket and shattered to bits. Esther braked beside him.

He moaned and used a plethora of profanity. Bone had split through one of his shins. Blood fled the wound in intermittent spurts. Esther could almost feel the injury herself. Thank God he'd had his helmet on.

Esther palmed her own phone and filmed the license plate as the truck pulled up to them. She now saw a symbol for *"POLÍCIA"* painted on the vehicle's side. Uniformed men soon stood before her.

"Leave us alone!" Esther screamed, thrusting the camera in their faces. "Please!"

Behind her, Mateo arrived on his ATV, as did his friends in their pickup. Brendan, in his suffering, didn't seem to notice that they were trapped.

"Why?" Esther wanted to know. "Why are you doing this?"

Mateo took one of his friend's guns and then approached the twins. He winked at the police officers.

"Please, no!" Esther begged. "Don't!"

Mateo stepped right onto Brendan's broken shin, digging in hard with his heel. Brendan yowled.

Esther sobbed. "Stop it! What do you want from us?"

Mateo smiled. *"Cállate, chica,"* he said.

He wrestled the helmet off her head and the phone from her hands. Esther clawed at him. Bit his wrist.

But she quickly lost the fight. Mateo tossed her helmet aside and threw the phone into the rainforest.

He then cracked the butt of the rifle against her skull.

After three consecutive blows, Esther passed out in the dirt.

When she awoke, Esther faced an azure sky dotted with cotton candy clouds. A gorgeous sight, really.

Too bad the air around her was stifling, broiling, and sweat plastered her clothes to her skin.

She soon realized: she was being dragged across an expanse of dark rock on a makeshift sled. Rope secured her to bamboo planks, pinning her arms and legs to her sides.

On her left, a pair of police officers pulled Brendan along, moaning, on a similar sled. On her right, Dad was tied to a sled, as well. He was alive, the bullet wound closer to his clavicle than to his heart.

Mateo and a friend towed Dad, grimacing with the task. Dad begged them, "Don't do this...Please...No..."

Mateo said, "Yes, Gabriel. To protect our people. *El Cherufe* commands."

Dad sobbed. "Me, then...Not the kids...Please...Please..."

Mateo shook his head. "All of you. He will be much happier this way."

Dad screamed, "Mateo, for the love of Christ, please!"

"Por el amor del Cherufe, Gabriel."

"What...What's happening?" Esther's tongue was heavy. It was difficult to think. To speak.

"They're going to kill us," Brendan whimpered. "Throw us in the fucking volcano! Sacrifice us or something!"

"You are gifts," Mateo said, "for the heart of our mountain."

That jumpstarted the synapses in Esther's brain.

WhatWhatWHAT???

She looked to her father. "Dad, he's joking, right? Dad!"

Dad didn't look at her. Just said, "I'm sorry, you two. For everything. I love you. I've loved you forever. I should've always been there. Been there for it all..."

Esther struggled against her binds. She wasn't going anywhere. None of them were.

She heard hissing. Distant rumbling, growing louder and louder.

"La puerta del Cherufe," said one of the officers. *"Hermosa."*

Mateo chuckled. *"Hambrienta. Ten cuidado."*

"It's not a door, Mateo!" said Dad. "It's a 'skylight'! Just a natural opening above the lava tube! Nothing more!" Dad winced. Raising his voice put him in a lot of pain.

Mateo snorted. "You haven't seen what we've seen. What our families have lived through for centuries. Last week's earthquake was a warning."

"Yes!" said Dad. "Of a possible eruption sometime in the future, but not...not of a...a *cherufe*! *Cherufes* are myths! Fiction!"

"*Lo siento, doctor*," replied Mateo. "*El Cherufe es la verdad de mi gente.* And he will punish us with fire unless he feeds."

The air grew warmer the closer they got to the red-hot opening in the earth.

"Don't!" Brendan screamed. "¡*Somos chilenos!*"

The locals laughed. One man said, "*Vosotros son mierdas.*"

His friend added, "*Comida del americano. Hamburguesas.*"

The others found that to be hilarious, too.

A minute later, they reached *la puerta del Cherufe*, a swimming pool-sized hole open wide above a growling river of lava. Steam whistled from within. Bubbles belched.

"Get us away from here, please!" Dad said. "The regolith... the ground...It's...it's not stable!"

Mateo said, "We do this fast, then." He nodded to his friend. "*Rápido.*"

Together, the two of them lifted Dad's sled into their arms. Esther and Brendan protested. Tears evaporated on their faces.

It wasn't fair! They'd just gotten Dad back! This was supposed to be their beginning, not their end!

Mateo looked into the volcano. "*Cherufe*, we give you life so that you give us ours."

Dad said, "Esther...Brendan...You're my—"

The bastards threw him—sled and all—into the fire. Dad wailed as the lava overtook him. After a few seconds, he mercifully fell silent.

"A snack," said Mateo. "Now, for *El Cherufe*'s favorite." He turned to Esther. "A virgin, like our ancestors used to provide."

"Fuck you!" Esther spat.

Mateo knelt down beside her and licked his lips. "*Deliciosa.*"

"Get away from me!"

Like it was any of his business, but Esther wasn't a—

"Hey, asshole!" Brendan shouted. "You want a virgin? I'm right fucking here!"

Esther screamed for him to stop. Her stupid, for-once-in-his-lifetime-noble brother. She couldn't lose him.

God, no! Not him, too!

Mateo told Esther, "You can be dessert."

Brendan nodded. "That's right, you fucker! Come over here!"

"Don't!"

"No, it's alright, Esther. Come here, you prick."

Mateo looked down at Brendan. "You die having never touched a woman? *Pobrecito.*"

"Was waiting for *tu madre, pendejo!*"

Mateo grinned. "Good one, *cabrón.*" He then punched Brendan in the gut.

Suddenly, the earth rolled. Rumbled. The men fell to their hands and knees, shouting in terror. A thunderous voice bellowed from below.

"*El Cherufe!*" someone shrieked.

The tremors continued as a massive beast emerged from the fire. It was forty feet tall, humanoid, made of magma. Vibrant, red eyes glowed inside its bright-orange, crocodilian head.

WHAT

THE

FUCK!!!

Everyone screamed but Mateo. He waved up to the creature. "*¡Hola, compadre!*"

The monster stared quizzically at its peons before reaching down and snatching a police officer inside a flaming claw. The lawman screeched as he was cooked alive in the creature's grasp.

"No!" Mateo pointed to Brendan. *"¡Por favor, come a los niños!"*

Esther said, "I don't think it's too picky, shithead!"

The *cherufe* tossed the blistered officer into its mouth and swallowed him whole.

The other men scrambled, including Mateo. The monster grabbed the fucker who shot Dad before he got too far out of reach. It tore the man in half and tossed both pieces down its gullet.

The behemoth then finally saw the twins lying at its doorstep. *ShitShitSHIT!!!*

"Don't look at us like that!" Brendan screamed. "Fuck you!"

"Try not to piss it off, Brendan!"

The earth trembled again. The *cherufe* peered off into the distance and roared.

A second monster exploded forth, creating a gargantuan new skylight in the regolith. Another *cherufe*, ready to eat, this one displaying the head of a puma.

Esther and Brendan watched as the puma cut off their captors' escape. With a giant paw, it crushed a policeman, sizzling him against the rocky terrain. With its other paw, it struck at the remaining officer but missed its target completely, accidentally caving in a chunk of the earth and sending the man, falling, into the fiery bowels of the mountain.

Mateo, another man, and the twins. All four trapped between a pair of magma monsters.

The crocodile hissed at the other *cherufe*. The puma growled back. It didn't seem like a friendly exchange at all.

The crocodile slunk back into the lava. The earth quaked before the beast re-emerged, this time directly beside the puma.

The titans battled, swiping and biting at one another. Apparently, there wasn't enough room in Cerro Verde for both of them.

The crocodile maneuvered around the puma's attack, clamping its enormous jaws around its enemy's neck, attempting to squeeze the life out of the cat. The puma yelped but managed to yank a jagged hunk of rock from the ground.

It raised the stone sword like Excalibur and stabbed it through the crocodile's throat. The reptile's eyes went wide, and it released its hold on the other *cherufe*.

The puma stood back from the crocodile, studying its opponent for a moment, before ripping the "sword" free and slicing it upward, severing the crocodile's jaws free of its face.

Molten blood spurted from the reptile's red-hot visage, raining down upon Mateo and his friend. Mateo dodged most of the flaming splashes, but his *amigo* took numerous hits to the body and engulfed in a blaze, died, meat charring on his bones.

The crocodilian *cherufe* collapsed, useless, back into the lava flow from whence it came.

The puma screeched at Mateo, who pleaded for mercy.

The creature chuckled as it pulled the man near, setting fire to his legs. Mateo howled as the puma brought its mouth close, ready to feed.

But it never ate him. Instead, it held its open jaws over Mateo, allowing globs of blazing drool to fall into his eyes and down his throat, melting the flesh off his screaming skull.

The puma then batted his smoking corpse aside and came for the children. It dove into the lava river and reappeared above the twins.

They, too, pleaded for mercy. The *cherufe* actually complied. It tore their ropes free. The monster's face morphed into their father's and smiled down at them, wistfully.

"The *fuck*?" said Brendan.

"Dad?"

DAD!

"Yes, it's me." The creature spoke in their father's voice, although it was a dozen times louder than before. "I think I've been chosen to be in charge now."

Holy shit!

What?!

WowWowWOW!!!

Brendan said, "You totally fucked those guys up."

The monster chuckled. "Not going to lie. It felt pretty great."

"There has to be more of them," Esther said. "Down at the village."

El Cherufe nodded. "I bet you're right."

Brendan asked, "You going to fuck them up, too, then? Erupt, I mean. Burn them down. You have to!"

The beast shook its head. "Doing so would destroy this place. Kill countless plants and animals. Not to mention plenty of good, innocent people. We got our revenge already, don't you think?"

"Yeah," said Esther.

Brendan shrugged. "If you say so."

Esther said, "And I don't really want anything bad to happen to the *pudús*, okay?"

She smiled up at the heart of the mountain. In a way, it felt like Dad ended up exactly where he'd always belonged.

He said, "I love this place. Always will. And someday, I hope to find that you've grown to love it, too."

Esther scooted over to Brendan and hugged him extra hard, giving him additional affection on their father's behalf. She wasn't sure that Dad would ever get to embrace his children again.

It certainly wasn't the new beginning that any of them had hoped for, but they would make it work, somehow. For the time being, at least, the Castillo family and the Cerro Verde volcano were at peace.

"My legs," Brendan said. "How am I supposed to get from here to a doctor?" He looked to his sister, gesturing to a sled. "You pulling me all the way?"

"I don't think so."

"Why the hell not? What other choice do we have?"

Ten minutes later, the twins clung to each other, screaming, as they surfed a slab of stone down the mountain on a controlled lava flow.

Evan Baughfman graduated with Honors in Creative Writing from the University of Redlands bachelor's program. Much of his writing success has been as a playwright, with many of his original plays finding homes in theaters worldwide.

He has also found success writing horror fiction, his work published most recently in anthologies by Black Hare Press, DBND Publishing, and Grinning Skull Press. Additionally, Evan has adapted a number of his short stories into screenplays, of which "The Tell-Tale Art," "A Perfect Circle," and "The Creaky Door" have won awards in various film festival competitions.

Evan's first short story collection, The Emaciated Man and Other Terrifying Tales from Poe Middle School, is now available through Thurston Howl Publications.

More information about Evan's writing can be found at amazon.com/author/evanbaughfman

DEBT

JOSEPH VALADEZ

"**Y**ou said it would be my turn next to choose the music, Dad!"

Astrid cranes her neck into the front seat of the black SUV with the fiery indignation that can only be produced by the young or deluded; Astrid, being 14 years old, falls into the former category.

Serena turns to quiet Astrid down, to soothe nerves that were on edge the moment they left for their "vacation," but Remy stops her. "She's right. It's fine."

Astrid smiles without understanding the interaction, without understanding the constant sacrifice that her parents live with; for her, the consequences of her father's eventual departure to hell are so far in the future that it may as well not exist.

The road is open, flanked by large evergreen trees, and the majestic monotony allows Remy's mind to wander into a place of danger, the danger of hope, the danger of courage.

For a moment, I was lost in the idea of taking a regular family vacation to a lake rather than receiving an order from the devil to report for duty: stupid.

"There it is, hun."

Serena points between a tightly packed wall of trees to a small opening that leads to a log cabin.

Remy stares dead eyed into the driveway as the truth of this trip settles, heavy and unrelenting, on his shoulders.

"Hun?"

Serena places her hand on Remy's strained forearm and watches the tension slip out of his body and deep into his heart; he merely shakes his head and pulls the car into the driveway.

"Go ahead and check out the cabin. I'm going to take a look around out back."

Before Astrid can find a way to join her father, Serena places an arm around her shoulders and herds her toward the front door, allowing Remy to walk around the back of the cabin alone.

He rests his head against the trunk of a tree and thinks back to the little church in the hospital, remembering the voice, the promise, the feeling of his entire life being swallowed up in a moment of dire need. His hand grips the tree tightly as he recalls praying for the life of his cancer ridden wife and unborn child; it only took a single thought, a single second, for the devil to find a home in his heart and offer a solution he could not pass up.

As the past threatens to drag Remy deeper into the bottomless chasm of this memory, his phone begins to giggle in his pocket. He looks down at the familiar number of Charles, his terse liaison to the devil, who tells him when and where "special" shipments need to be made; what is being shipped and to whom is ever a mystery to Remy who has no desire to taint the idea of his otherwise reputable business. Remy ignores the wriggling phone in his hand as long as he can until finally he taps the green button alight on the screen.

"The address is 90 Lake Shore drive."

"Always a pleasure to hear from you, Charles."

There is no response on the other end of the phone, so Remy tries to respond without childish contention. "I'll be there."

"Splendid."

In the snap of a finger, the soul of the phone is torn away and all that is left is the silent mass of electronics in his hand. Remy quickly goes back to the cabin, bids his family farewell, and drives back the way he came to meet Charles, the person he has spoken to often, but never actually met until today.

Remy drives until he sees a wood cutout of a bear that says "90 Lake Shore Drive." Taking a moment to be thoroughly impressed by the size of the home, he pauses before getting out of his SUV and walking up to the front door to ring the bell.

"Yes?" A voice rattles out of some hidden speaker and Remy looks up to find a camera.

"It's me."

"Who?"

"Remy."

"Remy who?"

He rests his head against the door. "Can you open the door?"

"Yes, I can."

Remy waits for a buzz or click, and when he does not hear it, he rattles the handle to find his entrance remains barred. "Will you open the door?"

"I suppose."

An electronic chirp sounds, and Remy pushes on the accommodating door that opens to a large foyer. Remy looks around waiting for his host to greet him.

"Stop standing in the foyer like a moron and come to the kitchen."

Is there no dignity even when paying the devil his due?

Remy follows the leash of a voice to the iron hand of a man that is wearing the "CEO on Vacation" starter pack complete with khaki shorts and flip flops. "Charles?"

The man is currently throwing random greens and other vegetables into a blender. "Indeed."

Remy timidly walks into the bright white kitchen and takes a seat on a barstool that would look more at home on a space station.

Charles makes eye contact, sets the blender to scream, then walks to place the surplus of items back into the fridge.

"Need a hand?" Remy hollers over the raucous blender which brings a selfish smile to Charles' face. He takes a moment to consider and then chooses to toss a few crumbs of his thoughts onto the countertop so that Remy can devour them greedily.

"You're going to have your hands full this week. Better rest while you can."

Whatever that means.

Charles turns off the blender, sets down two cups, and responds to Remy's thought.

"It means human sacrifice is a laborious task for the most practiced of us, so rest up."

Remy's heart seizes within his body, the world stops turning, and the only way he knows he's still alive is the discomfort of a dry mouth and shaky hands. "Did you just—?" Remy raggedly coughs, unable to continue his sentence.

"No, I didn't read your mind. Yes, I just said human sacrifice, and from the look on your face, it looks like management just sent me another cherry."

The eyes in Charles' head roll around with disbelief and irate wonderment as he fills up two cups with what looks like stagnant swamp water.

"I don't do...I'm not going..."

"You do now, and you will honor your contract, or it will be forfeit..."

Charles slides a glass of sludge toward Remy.

"...now I don't know if you read the fine print of the specific penalties of forfeiting your contract, but it's never pleasant. To your health?"

Charles shrugs, takes a sip of the green liquid, winces, then winks at Remy

"You can tell it's good for you because it tastes like liquified gutter trash. You're not drinking, Remy."

Remy puts the glass to his lips and drinks half of it before setting it down.

"Wow, you really take your health seriously."

Charles smiles without a care in the world and takes another measured sip from his own glass.

"Anything in this glass is going to taste better than what you're asking me to swallow."

"I'm not asking you to swallow anything lover. We just met." Charles blows him a kiss and laughs deeply to himself.

"But why now... It doesn't make any..."

Imbued with a single spark of feral rage, Charles slams his glass onto the countertop. "I get that it's your first time, but can we skip this? Can we skip the befuddlement, the bemoaning? I have one question for you: will you proceed, or will you breach your contract?"

Remy shrugs and looks around the spotless white kitchen with stainless steel appliances but finds nothing of use. "I really can't say what..."

Charles closes his eyes and puts up a hand. "Very simple. Proceed or breach. I want to hear one of those two words in the next ten seconds, or I will assume that you are non-compliant and wish to breach your contract."

It will mean the death of your wife, your child, and an eternity in hell as a traitor... "Five seconds."

Remy spews out his answer like fetid meat wriggling on his tongue. "Proceed."

"Sure?"

"Positive."

"I'm not going to have any trouble out of you, am I?" "Probably, but when the time comes, I'll get it done."

"We shall see."

Remy finishes what is left of the goo in his glass and shrugs. "Well, what's next?"

"Isn't it obvious, cherry? We kill."

"That's it?"

A warm laugh that feels like the smell of warm muffins cooking in the morning comes out of Charles. "I've distilled it, but that's the gist of it.

The drive to the cabin, to his family, is too short to give Remy the time to think, to repack all of the dirty laundry scattered across his heart.

The equation of saving three lives by taking one will never alleviate my heart from the burden of murder; I will have nothing left after I do this...

Returning for a moment, to the sad little pew in the church, Remy can hear his desperate voice reciting the words whispered to him.

"I shall not stray, shall not tarry, shall not disobey. I pledge my life, limb, and soul to thee."

Remy makes it back in time to find his family at the back of the cabin, watching the sun yawn down into the horizon. "Good meeting?"

Remy tilts his head and smiles a nauseous and wretched smile.

"Dad?"

Remy clears his throat and tries to look through them rather than at them.

"Yes, it was okay. Uh, I'm just tired is all and..."

"It's alright, hun. Maybe you should clean up."

Remy nods, turns around, but then turns back to them, losing the thread of the thought that Serena put in his head.

"Let me take you upstairs, sweetheart." She lovingly smiles at him, and he can feel black sludge roiling in his abdomen, threatening to rise and slither out of his throat.

I sacrifice for them so that they could turn around and sacrifice everything for me; they will lose their souls just for staying with me, and I will let them because I am weak and cannot bear to be alone.

"Serena..."

Holding his hand, she stops, and brushes her peppery blonde hair from her face so that he can gaze upon her angelic light brown eyes.

"Why won't you leave?"

It may be the desperation in his voice, but his question forces a single tear from her eye as she walks him up the stairs. Once in the bedroom, she closes the door and barrels a fierce finger into his chest. "I won't be having this conversation with you again, Remy! Even with this burden, we can be happy, if you allow it..."

Her frustration vibrates through her as she tries to maintain her composure and Remy can sense a great fracture freshly forming within her heart. She gently closes the door, and this is the thought and vision that rocks him into a strained sleep.

Remy drags a breath into his lungs and looks over to his wife to find her in her usual deep sleep. He checks his phone and finds a text message from Charles.

(Charles: Hey, you naughty little death badger. Meet me ASAP.)

Remy shakes his head and responds to the text with a clipped response.

(Remy: K)

He slides out of bed on his belly, tiptoes through the room to get dressed, and slithers down the stairs so as not to disturb the sweet slumber of the unafflicted. Before he leaves, Remy leaves a note upon the table explaining where he is headed and signs it with his love.

There are no coherent thoughts drifting through Remy's mind as he squirms down the twisted road; instead, what takes up a home in the center of his mind is the slow dull hum of the violent murder that he will have to commit. Before he knocks, Remy places his ear upon the door and hears a love song from the eighties being sung by Charles at the top of his voice. "Nothing compares to you..."

Remy shakes his head, knocks on the door, and waits for a voice but is instead greeted by the chirp of the unlocking door.

"Hey there, you sexy little murder grizzly. How'd you sleep?"

Remy looks at Charles but is unable to speak after the cannonball-like question is hurled at him. "Uh... um, fine I guess."

"Oh wow, that good huh? Did the wife try to peg you last night or something?"

"What! No, what?!"

Charles laughs again, jumps over the back of the white couch, and lays down, resting his head upon the palm of his hand like he's at a slumber party. "So, your first anal adventure, huh? Spill all the hot goss!"

Remy shakes his head and sits down on a white leather chair across from Charles.

"What is going on? Why are you acting like this? How did you go from clipped stoic to chatty Cathy?"

Charles rolls his eyes, sits up in a businesslike posture, and turns the music off. "Better?"

Remy widens his eyes and shrugs.

"Just because we are servants of the damned doesn't mean we can't be fun; besides I don't know what hell is like, but I think it is best to enjoy the time we have here before it's torn out and away from us. Right?"

If my wife and now my... boss?...leader?...sacrificial murder mentor?...says the same thing about my inability to enjoy what time I have left on this plane, then it must be me. The fault, the blame, is on my shoulders.

Remy shakes his head violently. "No!"

Charles raises his eyebrows and looks around the room for the person or persons that Remy must be arguing with. "Excuse me?"

"No! This is not my fault! It's not weird that I'm disgusted at the thought of murder. I should be reacting like this. This situation is not normal!"

Charles whistles and tilts his head back. "Sweet Satan's toenails, they sent me a live one. Of course, you're to blame. You're the one that signed the contract. The rest of us are just waiting for you to right the ship so that we can get on with our lives!"

Charles laughs and smiles in wonderment at the myopic scope of Remy's thought process. "You need a drink?

Remy nods. "Sugar or spice?"

Remy shrugs and finally answers. "Both."

Charles smiles and pours some whisky into a glass of coke and hands it to him. "Drink that down, you infuriating tart, and let's get started."

Remy downs the glass and Charles simply grins, rubs his hands together, and asks. "So, any preference for your first sacrifice?"

"I wouldn't know where to start. I mean... Do you just get a virgin or...?"

Remy struggles to find his way through this moment but quickly stills as he sees a disgusted sneer in the eyes of Charles. "Gross, Remy."

"What?"

"Virgins aren't necessarily pure. Besides, have you ever met an adult virgin? They're normally assholes. I attribute it to all the backed-up juices roiling and frothing inside of 'em, like an espresso machine without a pressure release valve..."

Charles nods to Remy as if they are sympatico.

"...then one day, POP, they explode..."

Charles shakes his head.

"...No, I'd keep away from virgins unless I absolutely needed one."

Remy wonders what one would "need" a virgin for and when or if he will ever "need" one. "Maybe you could just..."

Charles stops him with a magnanimous expression on his face. "Say no more. I think I can find something nice for your first time."

Remy sets his forehead between his palms. "It's not as if you're taking me to a brothel, Charles."

Charles shrugs. "We could do that after if you want. It's your first time and I want to make it special. Come on."

Charles walks Remy outside and opens the garage to reveal a forest green minivan with the back windows obstructed by dark black tint.

"There she is: the murder van, the murder mobile, the..." Charles struggles for a third nickname that can add some pizzazz to an otherwise dull mode of conveyance.

"Murder Machine?" Remy offers his submission like Oliver Twist and Charles laughs heartily.

"I love the alliteration and the reminiscent picture of those meddling kids."

Remy shrugs and smiles. "Now, who's got a hankering for some murder training?"

Charles shoves a stun gun into Remy's hand, and he holds it like a child, not yet able to talk, holds utensils for the first time. "What is this for?"

Charles rolls his eyes and slides the side door open; Remy peers inside with curiosity and disgust. "Where did you get the car seat and stuffed animals and why?" Remy allows himself to hope that Charles is domesticated in some way, but when he looks into his mentor's eyes, he knows this thought, this hope, is miles away from the truth.

"Camouflage, of course."

Charles runs Remy through the plan of coaxing the sacrifice into the back of the van and using the stun gun to incapacitate them long enough to get restraints and a gag on them. Charles tosses a lumpy plush gator at Remy's chest. "This is your murder buddy, abduction the alligator."

Remy shakes his head and looks under the belly of the gator whose stomach has a cut in it to facilitate the storing of zip ties, a gag, and the stun gun. "What the hell is wrong with you, Charles?"

"I thought you'd like your murder buddy..."

Charles rummages in the back seat, tossing other stuffed animals around the van. "...I have a platypus, a kangaroo. Oh, how about kidnapper the kangaroo..."

Charles shrugs his shoulders.

"...has a nice ring to it, right?"

Remy tucks the alligator under his arm. "The gator is fine."

Charles tilts his head to one side. "Who is fine?"

"Abduction, the alligator, is fine."

"There you go, Remy."

As Remy prepares himself for the dry run which will consist of Charles playing the part of the victim, he feels his phone squirming in his pocket and pulls it out.

"Not during work?" Charles flatly speaks to him from within the garage.

"It's my wife..."

"Make it quick."

Remy looks down at the screen like a child sneaking a peak at a text message during class.

(Serena: Hey Rem, got ur note, stepping out for some air. Left Astrid asleep at the cabin.)

(Remy: U okay?)

(Serena: Just needed some air. I'm fine.)

(Remy: Sorry about last night.)

(Serena: Thanx luv u)

(Remy: Luv u too.)

Remy grits his teeth and turns to walk into the garage.

"That good huh?"

"What?" Remy looks through Charles.

"Doesn't seem like the interaction was pleasant."

Remy's lips twist over one another. "So, you're not the only one I've been giving a hard time to in regard to his trip. I had a little meltdown in front of my wife last night. She was a little irritated and now she's off alone and left our daughter at the cabin."

"Oh."

That one word from Charles is full of images of imaginary screams ending in a dispassionate divorce. "It's not like that. She runs errands all the time without Ast... without our daughter, but this doesn't seem like a coincidence; she said she 'needed to get some air.' I'm fucking up every part of my life..."

"Hmm."

Remy was not sure what to expect, but the simple murmur seems inexcusable to him. "That's all?"

"What were you expecting, Remy?"

"The truth."

Charles doubles over and laughs. "I don't think so, Remy."

"I'm serious, Charles. Just tell me the truth."

Charles shakes his head and braces himself. "I'm not surprised that there is a strain on your marriage, and I'm not surprised at the struggle you exhibit to adhere to the terms of your contract."

"I told you I'll get it done, and I will, Charles."

"Maybe, but I can't be sure. You're a selfish person, and selfish people are not dependable."

"What?"

With genuine dismay, Remy looks at Charles with eyes widened and mouth agape. "You're selfish. You only ever think about how things affect you."

"That's not..."

"It is true. Have you thought about how this affects your wife, your daughter, or any of the other people that are trapped within your orbit? No! You only ever think about how people feel or act in relation to you." Charles turns and smiles so that he can punctuate his last sentence.

"You - are - selfish, Remy."

I'm not...I have sacrificed... granted no more than anyone else, but I did it with a pure heart, not for my own personal...

"Whatever."

Charles rolls his eyes. "Yes, whatever. Can we finish?"

Remy simply nods like the impetuous child that he is.

After they are done with the dry run, Charles closes the garage door and walks Remy back outside.

"Now what?"

Charles shrugs. "Now you go home, and I take care of a few things. I'll let you know when we are a go."

"That's it."

"For now."

Remy nods but is relieved to have some time with his family.

The rest of the day, the next morning, afternoon, and evening are penned in golden ink usually withheld for fairytales. Remy, his wife, and daughter, laugh, smile, and repair all the frayed cords of familial love so that Remy feels as though there is nothing he cannot do as long as he has that feeling, as long as he knows that he is loved.

Sitting on the porch, listening to the song of the creaking boughs of trees and the voices of those he loves the most, he feels his phone continually vibrating from a call. He looks down and sees the familiar number. "I have to take this."

He stands, and as he walks away, Serena presses her fingers against his forearm and feels his skin sliding away from her.

"Hey."

"Be at my house tomorrow at 12pm."

"Okay."

"No questions?"

"I mean, even if I have the answers to the questions, it won't change anything, right?"

"No, it won't."

"Then obsessing about it tonight is only going to ruin the rest of my evening."

"I like the new Remy. Let's hope he sticks around. See you tomorrow."

"12pm?"

"Exactly."

Charles' voice evaporates from the headset and is returned back to his body, wherever that may be.

Remy walks back out to the porch and sits down.

"Meeting with Charles tomorrow at eleven?"

Serena looks up and waits for her question to be answered.

"Twelve actually. How'd you know?"

"Lucky guess."

She smiles at him, he tries to smile back, and they both desperately cling to the feeling slowly slipping away, the feeling of the peaceful love that is billowing between them.

The next morning lacks any of the luster from the day before, and he can feel the loss as he disjointedly says goodbye to his family.

Remy feels comatose as Charles comes out of his cabin and greets him with an enlivened statement. "Well, in about an hour, we're going to abduct McKenzie; oh, she's the lovely little gas attendant that I picked out for you."

Remy's heart stops, but Charles does not allow the moment to settle; he stuffs everything in the minivan and shepherds Remy into the back seat.

During the ride, Charles tells him about the day prior. He describes going to the gas station, finding out McKenzie's shift based on the bathroom cleaning schedule, and devising the plan to pick her up on the way home, and Remy listens without understanding because he is lost to the eventuality of the future.

"She's going to come from the north, walk south, and sit on the bench. I'm going to be parked southeast. I'll drive around the corner to offer you a ride, and then I'll offer her a ride as well."

Charles parks, and Remy steps out of the van and takes a seat at the bus stop bench.

No, no, no, no!

Within five minutes, McKenzie walks up, gives him a quizzical but benign look, takes a seat, and to his surprise, he leans back, smiles, and nods at the woman who does the same. "To or from work?"

Whose words, whose voice, whose body is this because I know the voice, know the body, but the entity pulling the strings is foreign to me?

"Uhh." She looks around wondering how he knew.

"The uniform." She rolls her eyes with a "duh" expression and smiles again.

Be less sweet; be less naive.

"No, I just got off and heading home."

"Nice. So the rest of the night is yours to party hard."

She laughs and even her laugh is sweet and innocent. "You don't live here, do you?"

Remy smiles back at her. "You got me. No, I'm not from around here, but I might be relocating here."

A look of utter disbelief that someone would choose to move there parades across her face.

"You don't like it here?"

"It's fine, but I always thought this is a place where people are born, not a place that people move to; I guess everyone wants to be somewhere else. Why are you moving?"

"It's kind of a long story."

"I've got nothing but time."

Just as Remy prepares to answer, Charles pulls up. "Hey man!"

Remy looks up and tries to mimic authentic surprise. "What are you doing here?"

Charles smiles. "I told you I would try to pick you up if I could, and I was able to."

Remy walks up to the passenger side windowsill down at his alligator who is glaring back at him with disapproval.

Charles whispers. "Keep going."

"What are all these stuffed animals doing here?"

"Just dropped the kiddos off. You can toss em in the back."

As Remy is moving the stuffed animals, Charles leans over and waves to McKenzie who waves back without one untrusting speck in her eyes.

Remy slides the door closed, talks to Charles in a hushed voice, and then turns around. "Do you want a ride?"

I am the epitome of innocence; I am the lamb; I am the cherub.

McKenzie looks at Charles, then Remy, and as they can feel her receding, Charles jumps in. "It's no trouble, but if you want to wait for the bus, I won't be offended."

McKenzie kneads her hands, thinks for a couple seconds, but in the end, she bounds to her feet and smiles with gratitude as she enters the van.

"Can you see if my garage opener fell on the side of your chair? My lady will kill me if I lose another one of those remotes."

This is the signal for Remy to pull the lever that lowers the back of his seat to trap her and then turn and taze her in the neck. Remy's hand slips between the door and the seat and his slimy fingers grip onto the handle, and the back of his chair falls as it is supposed to fall, but all of the stillness, all of the resolve he felt at the bus stop bench vanishes when he turns and is face to face with McKenzie and her doe eyes.

"That seat has been giving me trouble. You just have to pull it again." The voice of Charles calmly sails over to Remy.

"Come on, man. You're going to crush that poor girl."

"Maybe I could help." The words roll out of her mouth like weary toddlers practicing tumbling.

"Do it!"

Charles sends a fist into Remy's side and the shot of pain puts him to action. He turns, tazes her, and feels a cold gelatinous death twist in his stomach as her eyes widen, dull, then close.

Calmly and almost with a soothing edge, Charles speaks slow and steadily to him. "Are you going to be able to bind her, or should I?"

Just as they practiced, Remy crawls over the center console and disembowels the alligator. Her arms and legs are bound, mouth is gagged, but all of her pure orange sunset innocence cannot be muted, cannot be bridled.

"Put this over her face. It will help when she wakes up."

Remy takes hold of the black cotton pillowcase and slides it over her head.

Remy does as he's told and then creeps into the third-row seat to lay down, to curl up with all of the grotesque images of himself dancing through his head.

The drive, the silence, the trees waving goodbye to Remy's sanity, all make the trip move faster, make every moment feel supercharged so that Remy feels as though he will burst, as though he were a meteorite rushing through the atmosphere fighting against the fissures and cracks, threatening to splinter him into dust.

Charles pulls the car off the winding road and parks it behind the low branches of a tree.

"Get her and follow me." Charles grabs a small bag and slips out of the car and into the lazy light of dusk.

Lift your leg, extend it, take your other leg, extend it, move past the trees, that branch cut into my cheek...

Remy follows Charles deeper into the woods, and though the sun is not moving any faster, the deeper they trudge into the woods, the darker it seems. The closer they get to their destination, the more sinister the leaves upon the trees appear.

They reach a clearing, and after Remy sets Mackenzie down upon a round flat stone, he looks around the circular clearing where the trees lean away from the stone, leaning away from the cursed land.

"Here you go."

Charles hands Remy a knife that is six inches in length with a wooden handle that feels and looks as though it has been a part of this knife for a hundred years; it is not intricate or expertly crafted, but it feels strong and wails into the dusk just like Mackenzie is about to.

"What am I supposed…"

"It doesn't matter how she dies as long as she dies on the stone with that knife."

"But how…"

"I can't tell you that. I can only say that her blood must be spilled by that blade and that it must fall upon the altar."

Charles nudges him with a hand upon his lower back, and Remy tentatively moves closer to Mckenzie who is convulsively crying without a mask to cover her twisted face.

There is no apology that can overshadow the monstrous evil that I am about to pass onto you. To say anything to you would be to disrespect you further.

Remy grips hold of the knife as if it is the only thing keeping him from falling to his death and just as he is about to send it swiftly into her flesh, he locks eyes with her, cuts her bonds and screams, "Run!!!!"

She doesn't get more than a few steps before the gods release a sound of thunder that echoes throughout the forest. Remy sees her body drop and turns to see Charles holstering a gun back under his shirt.

"Just as I thought."

Charles shakes his head as he flicks his eyes to signal Remy to turn around and behold the fate that he molested. He turns and tries to run toward Serena who has appeared from the opposite end of the forest, but he is bound by some invisible power that has rendered his limbs useless. He cannot say how, but he knows it is coming from Charles.

"Serena!!!"

She doesn't speak: she simply walks past him, picks up the knife that he dropped to the ground when he cut Mackenzie's restraints, and softly steps onto the altar.

"Astrid deserves to live and to have a parent to care for her. You've sacrificed enough."

"You can't. It won't make a difference!!!"

Remy continues to struggle against the power clamping down around him like a snake because he is not capable of understanding the love and selflessness that Serena possesses.

"I know you better than you know yourself, sweetheart, and I knew this was beyond you and love you for it. I made my own deal with the devil while you were with Charles, and payment is due now."

Serena takes the knife, slits both of her wrists, drives the blood coated blade quickly into her neck, and collapses to the ground; her lips grope for air like a fish cast onto land and then she stops, ceases to exist, and with her goes the world.

There are screams, there are the lamentations of the damned, but what Remy lets loose from the shadowed depths of the chasm where once there was a soul is a roar that echoes throughout the entirety of the forest, quieting every living creature, not out of fear, but out of some primal understanding, some shared loss that they can all feel.

Last Chance

Laura Kaschak

I don't know why I agreed to this. Driving out to the middle of nowhere in Pennsylvania and spending an entire weekend at a lousy bed and breakfast is not my idea of a good time. Unfortunately for me, it is my wife's idea of a good time. And since she's gotten all melodramatic again, I have to do stupid shit like this for a while until she is appeased, and things can go back to normal.

She's calling this weekend our "last chance at being happy" and saving our marriage. Women just love to put a theatrical spin on everything. It's not that big of a deal. She's pissed at me for getting carried away when I was angry. It was just a few small bruises. It's not like I've ever punched her in the face or anything. Not that I haven't wanted to do exactly that at times. But I control myself even when she is being crazy. She's lucky I have more self-control than she does. If she didn't fight me so hard, she wouldn't end up with those tiny bruises she makes such a big deal out of.

You'd think she'd learn by now not to push my buttons. She knows when I get mad that she should just shut up and stop aggravating me. No matter how many bruises she ends up with, she keeps pushing me every single time. But she won't ever admit that she is the one who makes me lose my temper. She never takes responsibility for anything she does. It's always all my fault.

"Turn right up there," she tells me.

"Where? I don't see a street sign or even a road that way." I shouldn't have let her hold the directions.

"Just slow down. My mom's friend said it's easy to miss. There it is—just after that big tree."

I hit the brakes, spraying dirt and rocks along the side of the car. Great, I just washed it yesterday for this trip. Not that she'd ever appreciate or even notice that or anything else I do. We've been on these dirt roads for at least an hour. I don't know how any business could stay open this far from civilization.

"What is the name of this place again?" I ask her.

"The Cozy Cottage. My mom said it would be the perfect spot for us. Her old college friend owns and runs it. She said she'll take good care of us."

I have to stifle a groan. "Since when is your mom interested in doing anything nice for me? Wasn't she the one telling you not to come back to our home and to walk away from this marriage?"

Her mother always sticks her nose in our business, and it drives me crazy. Of course, Gemma encourages it by running to her every time we have the slightest disagreement. I think she just likes having her mom to gang up with and make me look like the bad guy.

She continues to stare out the front window. "She just wants me to be happy. That's all. She set it all up for us because she knows I'll be a lot happier if we do this."

I know what would make me happy: if her mother dropped dead. But I'm not going to say anything because I'm supposed to be on my best behavior as we "give this a real try."

I start to see part of a building through the trees. God, please don't let this run-down old shack be where I'm staying all weekend.

"There it is," she calls out. "It's just like my mother described."

"You have got to be kidding me, Gemma. I have to waste my whole weekend at this place? I honestly don't know how you can be so stupid sometimes. Why did I let you pick? You can't do anything right."

She looks down at her lap, and I realize I messed up. I forgot how overly sensitive she can be. Even when she is being stupid, she expects me not to point it out. But I don't know how else she's going to learn to use her head if I don't tell her.

I reach over and take her hand. "Hey. It's fine. We brought that nice bottle of scotch with us, and at least we won't have to deal with any crowds, right?"

I smile at her, hoping for one back, but it's clear she's going to use this as an excuse to pout. But finally, she lets out a big sigh and the corners of her mouth turn up a little bit even though her lips stay tight together.

"You're right. I knew you might be a bit disappointed when you saw it. But I'm telling you, this is just what we need to make everything better. Please just give it a try, Dan. Okay? You'll see why I picked this place. It's really supposed to be a special experience."

I know the less I say, the faster we can get this over with and move on with our lives, so I decide to keep my thoughts to myself. I am so grateful I brought that scotch.

The front door swings open as I put the car in park. A short, chubby woman wearing a flower covered muumuu waddles out the door to wave at us. I'm surprised the old bat could even hear the car pull up. She looks a lot older than Gemma's mom.

I glance over at Gemma, but she's just grinning and waving back like an idiot. She jumps out of the car and runs up to the old woman. I walk around to the trunk to start unloading our bags and get a good look at my weekend prison.

It looks like one of those old two-story Victorian houses but without any of the charm. At one time, it must have been painted in the obnoxious pink color of a toddler's beauty pageant dress, but time and neglect have stripped most of it away leaving behind grey weathered wood with chips of old pink paint clinging between crumbling planks.

Gemma comes over to grab one of the bags, and I whisper to her, "I thought you said this was a bed and breakfast. There's no way they've seen a customer here since before we were born." She shoots me a look I know all too well. This weekend is getting longer by the minute.

The smell of mothballs, mold, and old lady perfume hits me before I even reach the door.

"Well, hello there dear. You must be the mister. You can call me Mary," she wheezes out to me.

"Yes, nice to meet you, Mary. I'm Dan. Thanks so much for making room for us here." I say that as if there was any possibility they could have been booked up. But I'm the only one who gets the joke.

She leans her head toward me, cupping a hand around her ear. "I'm afraid you're going to have to speak up, dear."

I roll my eyes and repeat myself louder. At least I won't have to worry about her hearing us doing all our "making up" tonight.

"Oh, of course. Anything for my old friend, Joanne. How is your mother doing these days, dear?"

I duck out to grab the last bag instead of having to listen to boring drivel as the women chitter back and forth like a couple of hens. They're still droning on by the time I come back.

"Well then!" I say loudly. If I don't do something, we'll be on this rotting porch all day. "I'd love to see our room and get these bags put down. Lead the way, Mary."

"Oh yes. I'm sorry. What am I thinking? You're not here to listen to an old lady blather away. Of course, come this way."

I ignore a death glare from Gemma and follow behind Mary. The inside is worse than the outside. I can't believe people like this exist outside of a Tweety Bird cartoon. Every available surface has a doily on it. The furniture and rugs all have giant flower prints. She even has those big-eyed kid paintings on the walls. I swear this must be a joke. I'm starting to wonder if Gemma purposely chose this place as part of my punishment.

Mary chatters away at us, shuffling along at a pace that gives me road rage even though I'm not in a car. Finally, we reach our door. I quickly shove Gemma inside and say our thanks. I shut the door before Mary can respond.

Gemma is standing with arms crossed and a sour look on her face.

"What? We need to be alone to reconnect, right? I just want to be with you. Mary understands that. It's fine."

She softens a bit, but the arms stay crossed. I walk over to wrap my arms around her and nibble on that spot on her neck I know she loves. No one can melt her like I do. I feel the tension leave her body.

"So, what do you think about checking out the trails?" she asks.

I pull back and blink at her a few times, trying to understand what she's talking about.

"You weren't listening to her at all, were you?" she says with a chuckle. "Mary said the property is surrounded by beautiful hiking trails. She says this time of year we're likely to spot some deer or other wildlife. Want to take a walk before it gets too dark?"

Walking wasn't really the activity I had in mind, but I guess I'm still paying my dues. "Sure, why not? I'm guessing there aren't many other things to do around here."

The trails actually turn out to be nice. Gemma seems happy, and she really is beautiful when she smiles like this. I get a little lost looking at the way the setting sun is making her hair glow around her when a rancid smell stops me in my tracks.

There's no mistaking the scent of death and rot. I look around for the source. Gemma must have caught a whiff too because her hand goes over her nose and mouth. A buzzing sound to my right turns my attention. I push aside some branches and discover a clearing.

The sound of flies swarming is almost as overwhelming as the putrid stench. Scattered across the ground are various body parts from small animals. The parts are small enough to make it difficult to tell what animals they used to be, but a chunk near me looks like it might have been a rabbit foot.

"There must be some predators out here. Maybe we should head back." Gemma pulls on my arm.

"But look, nothing is chewed or torn. They all look like they've been sliced clean to me." That's when my eyes drift up to notice the bodies hanging from a tree branch. The rabbits' eyes bulged from the twine wrapped around their necks. Their bellies have been sliced down the middle, leaving entrails dripping down to create blackened puddles under them. I point it out to Gemma, "No animal did that."

"Well then we *definitely* should head back." She gives my arm a harder yank and this time I go with it. We rush back to the house.

Mary is puttering around the kitchen when we return. She quickly dismisses our questions about what we discovered in the woods as being regular hunter castoffs or animal attack leftovers. I'm not sure she really heard what we said. There's no point in pressing it. She's as dumb as she looks.

"Well, you kids have fun. I'm off to bed. Help yourselves to anything you need."

It's early but getting to our bedroom sounds like a great idea to me. We say our goodnights and retreat to our room. Thankfully, the bathroom is attached so we don't have to go into the hallway and risk any more elderly chats.

Gemma hops in the shower as I pour myself some scotch. A white streak outside the window catches my eye. It's moving between the trees, so I only catch glimpses at first. When it reaches a small clearing, I get a clearer look before it continues to the next group of trees. And now I really wish I hadn't looked. Mary is stark naked, romping through the forest.

"Gemma! Gemma, you have to see this. Come here," I call to her as she steps out of the bathroom wrapped in a towel. She comes over to the window and looks where I'm pointing. It takes a minute, but Mary emerges with arms waving at the sky, large sagging ass waving toward the ground as she bounces through the woods.

Gemma laughs. "Oh my! Well, my mom did mention that Mary was a sort of 'free spirit' type when they went to school together. Part of the reason they lost touch was Mary's interest in alternative lifestyles. My mom will get a kick out of this when I tell her. Let's just close the blinds and leave her to whatever that is."

I have to work hard to get that image out of my head. Talk about a boner killer. But I really did miss Gemma these past couple weeks. Everything else is quickly forgotten as I get her into bed. We have a lot of time to make up for. I don't waste another minute.

I stir awake, thinking I might have heard something, but in my sleepy haze, I can't be sure what it was. I pick up my watch on the nightstand and see it's 3:00 AM. I lay back down and find the pillow next to me is empty.

"Gemma?" I call out. The bathroom light is off, and the room is silent. With all the creepy things that have happened since we've been here, I don't like the idea of her wandering around alone at night. It's just like her to ruin my sleep on my vacation. Now I have to get out of bed just because she doesn't have the sense to stay put in a place like this. I go looking for her, reminding myself that when I find her, I'm not supposed to point out what an idiot she is.

I'm tiptoeing down the stairs when I notice a soft humming sort of noise. I realize it sounds like voices murmuring together, but I can't make out what they're saying. I call out quietly to Gemma again but get no answer. I follow the sound of the voices.

They get louder as I approach a door toward the back of the kitchen. I press my ear against it but still can't quite make out what's being said. There is a repetitive, melodic quality to the sound. I'm thinking it's a radio or TV and wonder if I shouldn't explore further in case Mary is doing a late-night rumba in the nude.

I turn to look elsewhere when another voice rises above the murmurs. This voice sounds a lot like Gemma to me. Now I open the door to see a dark staircase that leads down into what must be a basement. The voices are louder now, and I listen closely for more signs that Gemma might be down there.

I head down the stairs into the basement. It's the old kind of cellar with a dirt floor and stone walls. The earthy scent of the floor mingles with burning candle wax. I can see the flames flickering in a doorway near the back of the cellar.

I walk to the candlelight where I can now tell the voices are in fact chanting together. It doesn't sound like it could be coming from a recording, and I'm disturbed to think we haven't been as alone in this house as we'd thought. I notice there are strange markings written in the dirt on the way to the door. Similar markings have been painted on the walls in a reddish-brown color.

I creep up to the edge of the doorframe and peek in. The room is much larger than it seems would be possible under a house of this size. I realize then that it's not really a part of the house but instead seems to be a sort of cave that was dug into the earth.

The room is filled with candles lighting up a group of naked people standing in a circle, arms raised in the air with eyes closed. In the middle of their circle is a large symbol, a lot like the ones I saw on the walls. Right in the center I see Gemma, down on her knees. Her head is bowed, hands resting on her legs.

Without thinking, I call out her name. The chanting abruptly stops as all eyes turn toward me.

"Get the hell away from her," I snarl but before I can finish my threat, a pain explodes in the back of my head and the world goes black.

I'm groggy when I first begin to regain consciousness. Panic quickly clears my head as I realize I can't move my arms or legs. My limbs are stretched out wide, legs parted far enough to make my groin ache. The skin around my wrists and ankles burns as it rubs against the restraints. I can lift my head just enough to look down at my naked body strapped to a table. The chanting surrounds me. In the candlelight, Gemma steps into view and leans over me.

She's smiling. Why the hell is she smiling?

"Hi, Dan. I promised you a special experience, didn't I?" She seems downright giddy.

"What are you doing, Gemma? What is this?" I'm trying to sound angry, but my voice comes out pathetic and weak. That's even more humiliating than having my body exposed.

"It really was nice of Mary to offer her place to us. When my mother told her about our situation, she was happy to help. Of course, she is getting something in return. Her group needed a new offering. I don't know all the details of their rituals. That's not important to me. What is important is that you will never put another bruise on me again. I can walk away from this and be truly happy. Just like my mom wants for me. I told you this weekend would be my last chance for happiness."

In my peripheral, I see Mary and the others writhing as they cry out in unison, over and over. They are getting more feverish in their movements and chants. Mary is holding up a large knife in one hand and a golden chalice in the other. She breaks away from the chant and starts talking to the air. It's hard to make out her whole speech over the sound of my heart pounding and the voices of the group. But I know I hear the words "summon" and "sacrifice."

"You're crazy. You're all completely insane! Let me off this table, goddammit!" I strain as hard as I can back and forth, but the ropes aren't loosening at all.

Gemma shushes me and slides her hand along the side of my face. "Aw, poor Dan. It must be so hard to not be in control for once. To feel helpless." She pauses and smiles to herself. "I know you thought you were much too smart to ever end up in a situation like this. But you should be proud of me. You always said I couldn't do anything right. And maybe you had a point. After all, I did marry you. Well, I finally got something right." With a grin, she steps back away from the table until I can no longer see her.

I'm drenched in sweat as I continue to twist pointlessly against the ropes. The chanting grows louder, but I can no longer see the people from where I'm lying. I helplessly stare up at the candle flames creating shadows on the ceiling.

I feel the knife cut deep into the flesh between my legs, and the world is drowned out by searing pain and the sound of my screams. A massive horned shadow rises up the wall and onto the ceiling above me. A loud growl tears through the room and rumbles the table I'm strapped to.

My struggles weaken as warm blood puddles underneath me and drips to the floor. I find myself grateful to be slipping away as the horned shadow solidifies and draws closer to me. A pair of orange glowing eyes appear in the shadow just before everything goes dark.

Laura Kaschak

Laura Kaschak was born and raised in the pine barrens of New Jersey where she spent most of her youth hanging with the Jersey devil. Now she is a wife and mother of two in Virginia successfully fooling everyone into believing she is a grown up. When she's not writing, she's work o her latest art creation or Halloween costume, teaching her parakeet new words, or cuddling her pug.

STURDY COMFORT

W. T. PATERSON

They stood in the rain spattered with blood. Abdel grinned a toothy smirk at Florence, the machete poking out of the ground like a steam engine lever.

"Hive bee-n waiting," he said, rising to his feet. The mask across his face demanded more.

"Honey, I'm home!" Florence said.

"The weather today is...swarm," Abdel said

"Your final grade is a BEE," Florence said.

"So that's what all the BUZZ is about," Abdel said.

"That's what happens when you don't bee-hive," Florence said.

They looked at the prone body by their feet as the flashing blues and reds of an emergency crew approached. The bubbled and boiled flesh turned the corpse into something that more resembled a monster than a human.

"I think I love you," Abdel said, pinching Florence's fingers as a voice shouted, "Hands where I can see 'em!"

"Your honor, given the situation and Mr. Sinclair's clean record, previous events not withstanding, I move to enroll my client in *Sturdy Comfort*," the public defender said, his sleepless, hollow eyes sagging toward a loose tie. The honorable Judge Diana McMillan looked over the case file. Abdel Sinclair. Aggravated Assault. Six months served. Attacked three bouncers the night after his tech startup *Prymal* failed to secure series C funding. CEO disappeared with millions, Abdel fingered as the company scapegoat.

"Well, no previous record. I imagine we'll never get the full story," McMillan said.

"There's an opening in Tamworth, New Hampshire to rebuild a campsite after the...um...1980's tragedy."

"The Masked Killer case? Campers all hacked up?" McMillan asked.

"Unfortunately yes, your honor."

McMillan contemplated for only a moment before agreeing. Less than 24-hours later, a young Deputy with a sleeve of tattoos and trendy hair, and Florence LaMontagne, the new owner of the campsite property, picked up Abdel Sinclair from Manchester Airport.

A recent divorcé, Florence had long auburn hair that feathered out at the ends and light brown eyes.

"Once built, I'll be able to rent it out for yoga retreats, weddings, company outings, things like that," she said.

Abdel noticed her flawless complexion, the type of woman worth changing for, a different breed, a rare catch writhing with hidden pain.

"I like your skin," he said, hands bound by a plastic pull-tie. Evergreens whipped by, the radio pulsing with low volume static.

"I'll uh...I'll stay on site," the Deputy said, and then looked into the rearview mirror with *what's your deal, bro?* eyes. Then, he smiled at Florence like everything was cool. Abdel didn't appreciate it. When he briefly dozed off, Abdel dreamt of tying the Deputy to a chair with plastic pull-ties and shaving the trendy haircut into a skunk stripe.

The site itself was set against Lake Lumber, named after the fabled New England explorer Luscious Lumberjack, who many saw to be a cheap knock-off Paul Bunyan. At one point, an internet campaign tried to raise money to persuade law-makers to rename the area Lake Blood, but the town rallied and ultimately prevented the change.

Twelve small cabins sat unused across the seven acres of land. The roofs had holes, the walls needed mending, and the steel bunks inside were rusted beyond rehabilitation. It looked like they hadn't been touched since the crime scene investigators wrapped up shop. Trees had fallen from storms making it nearly impossible to pitch tents inside of the flat land, and orange pine needles cushioned the ground as thick as a mattress. Whatever trails had existed were reclaimed by the forest's overgrowth.

The Deputy's SUV could only travel so far down the dirt road before they had to park and hike the mile and a half to the central building that was only recently set up with elec-tricity, plumbing, heating, and wifi. A short man with a pot-belly, long silver hair, and gray beard down to his waist waited. He wore cargo shorts that only covered the top of his thighs and a blue tank top, even though the temperatures were in the low fifties.

"Hallo!" the man said, waving from the roof of a sleep-away cabin while holding long silver nails between his teeth. Climbing down, he trotted over to formerly shake hands. "My name is Jeffery Jouster, rehabilitated con and master craftsman. You can call me Joust or Jouster, just don't call me late for waterskiing!"

The Deputy nodded with familiarity, stepped aside for Florence, and then swatted nervously at some bees. Florence shook Joust's hand.

"I appreciate everything you've done so far," she said.

"Ain't you a shining beacon," Joust said. "You single?"

"Recently divorced and not actively looking."

"I'm Abdel," Abdel said, holding both hands in front of him still bound by a white plastic pull-tie.

"Still got you tied up, I see. There ain't no need for that," the short man scolded. He folded his arms and shot daggers into the Deputy who pulled a spring-loaded blade from his utility belt and cut Abdel free.

"Thanks."

"I don't care what your history is or what you've done. What I do care about is teaching you valuable life skills through the rehabilitation of this camp. Maybe somewhere along the way, you get rehabilitated too."

Abdel stared at Joust wondering what it would take to never have to talk to him again.

"I used to be a coder, so construction is new to me," Abdel said.

"Do you do websites?" Florence asked.

"Are lambs brought to slaughter?" Abdel asked.

"Not always..." Florence said, shrinking back.

"Exactly. But for you, absolutely."

"But first," Joust interjected, "I show you the tools! We have machetes for the overgrowth, rusty chainsaws that need some TLC, nail guns, real guns, saws, gasoline, pretty much every dang thing to rebuild...your life."

Abdel followed Joust to a shed protected by a crooked door held up by a broken padlock.

"Smells in here," Abdel said, stepping into the shed.

"Yeah, that's all these decaying leaves on the ground. Needs a good sweeping. Does give it a nice aroma, though."

They grabbed the tools and trekked to cabin six where they worked for the entirety of the day patching up the roof. When Abdel hammered some roof beams into place, Joust said, "Nailed it! I'm beaming!"

When they deconstructed a metal bed frame and rebuilt one out of reclaimed wood, Joust said, "Tonight, you sleep on your own success."

When they cooked dinner over a firepit and Florence wandered by wearing a fleece pullover and hiking shorts, Joust whispered, "My software just turned into hardware," and wouldn't stop giggling.

As he slept in the cold bunkhouse atop his own success, Abdel could feel something inside of him stirring.

In his dreams, he roasted Joust over an open flame while Florence feasted, blood spilling from her mouth, overlooking Lake Lumber.

It was on the third day that Abdel found the mask. Cabin six had been completed, and he was midway through cabin seven's repairs, which meant sanding down the floors and applying varnish while Joust worked on the electrical.

Abdel was taking a breather when he noticed a piece of the knotty pine wall jutting out farther than the rest. He pushed at it with his callused fingertips. Something was blocking the wall from the inside.

Abdel reached his hand inside and felt the curve of something wooden. His fingers hooked inside of two slits, and he yanked the item away.

It was a carved totem. That was the word he thought of, totem, because it seemed too small to be worn across the face like a mask even though it had holes for the eyes and mouth. The nose jutted out in a sharp wooden triangle. Squiggled circles and jagged lines connected and drifted into two separate designs that almost seemed like the world was bleeding.

Abdel walked to a bathroom mirror speckled with black rust and white paint and held the mask up to his face. The cabin got cold, and out over the lake, a thunderhead boomed. *Awaken*, a voice in his head growled as a swarm of bees started pelting the window. Joust hollered from the roof and told the insects to *git outta here!* The moment the mask touched his skin, visions blasted into his brain.

A body of a man was doused with gasoline and lit on fire. Voices shouted to just *jump into the lake*. Murky water filled his lungs.

Time passed.

The body emerged from the lake and dismembered the camp staff with an axe and chainsaw. He carved the mask to hide his horrific burns while reciting ancient incantations under a thunderstorm. He hid the mask in the wall, stepped outside with a machete, and was immediately electrocuted by a lightning bolt.

"Can relate," Abdel said, pulling the mask away from his face. The moment he did, the sun came back out, and a symphony of forest creatures resumed their songs. Joust began hammering again.

For the rest of the day, Abdel found that he was aware of everything on site that could be used as a deadly weapon.

"Y'all are making some progress!" Florence said, smiling and holding handmade sandwiches for lunch. "Hungry?"

"Starving," Abdel said. He had been using a machete, *the* machete, to clear growth from the paths. To remove the rust and flecks of dried blood, he dipped the blade into some consumer grade acid from the utility shed.

"Where's Joust?" she asked, craning her neck.

"Testing a toilet in bunkhouse two," Abdel said.

"He'll eat later then. I've been meaning to talk to you. How are you settling in?"

Abdel wasn't sure how to explain what he had been feeling over the past week. He looked at Florence. She was wearing a grey college sweatshirt from UMass Dartmouth and faded blue jeans tucked into brown hiking boots. On the ground, a hairy black spider the size of a Girl Scout cookie crept toward her feet.

Kill... the voice said, and without thinking twice, Abdel raised the machete up over his head and launched it toward Florence's feet. The blade landed dead center through the spider's back.

"Whoa!" Florence said, doubling over. "Did you see the size of that thing? I hate spiders."

Abdel pulled the machete out of the ground and watched the spider slide off into two chunks.

"Me too," he said.

"Is it weird that I don't feel bad? I know it was just a spider being an innocent spider, but another side of me is like *burn in Hell, evil creature.*"

"Everyone is guilty of something," Abdel said and wiped the machete off on the side of his pants.

They walked to a nearby picnic table that Florence had been setting up. The orange pine needles had been cleared, and fresh gravel crunched under the weight of each footstep. Birdcalls echoed over the still lake that lapped against the shore with the breeze. Spring was in full bloom, and the smell of the wood in the surrounding pines reminded them that they were far away from city life.

Florence sat down first and held up two saran wrapped sandwiches.

"Turkey or...turkey?" she asked.

"You wouldn't happen to have turkey, would you?" Abdel asked. Florence blushed. She handed him the sandwich from her right hand.

Say thank you... the voice in his head roared.

"Thank you," Abdel said.

"My pleasure," Florence smiled. "I'm sorry I haven't been as available as I probably should be. I've been wanting to pick your brain for a bit, but as you can see, lots of work to be done."

Commend her on her hard work... the voice boomed.

"Your hard work has paid off. I'm impressed."

"Oh, thank you, oh my goodness. That's very kind of you. Sorry if this is TMI, but it's been incredibly helpful to have *something* to do. I swear I'm not crazy, but keeping my mind occupied on something other than the div..." and she paused.

"I was almost married once," Abdel said. "But she um, she cheated on me with my boss. And I kept working for my boss Billy, even after breaking it off with my ex. We'd see each other all of the time still, but it was like we were strangers, like we'd both become different people. Then my boss skipped town with her and all of the company's assets to the Cayman Islands or something, and I'm the one who got arrested."

"I'm so sorry," Florence said. "If you don't mind me asking..."

"Fight broke out the day everything really went south. Drank too much. Had a lot bottled up, I guess. I'd never been violent before. Ever. It didn't feel like me."

"I know what you mean," Florence said, staring across the lake. "Held too much inside. Letting it out felt..."

"Liberating?" Abdel asked.

"Yeah..." Florence said. "Cleansing, even."

In the distance, Joust and the Deputy laughed as they walked toward the picnic area.

"Here comes the fun brigade," Abdel said.

"Not a fan?" Florence asked. She nudged his foot under the table. "Between you and me, that Deputy is a creep. I caught him watching me dress through my window once. Said he was out on patrol."

Eliminate the threat, the voice in his head roared. A flash of vision showed a saw, beam, tarp, and rope. *Blind him...*

"I can build you some blinds," Abdel said. "Won't take long."

"Really? I would love that!" Florence said. "Head over around 7 tonight, if that works? Do you like wine? I have wine, and maybe we can talk about the website, and life, and...I'm sorry, I'm getting ahead of myself."

Tell her this, the voice in his head said, and then whispered like a secret.

"As long as you're there, it'll be all I need."

"It's a date," Florence said. "I mean...it's a time. We'll have a time. You know, we'll just chill. Netflix and chill. Not what I meant."

Florence stood up from the wooden picnic table and hurried away. As she passed Joust and the Deputy, she waved from her hip and told them to eat up.

"Are you on the menu?" the Deputy asked.

"Dude, weak," Joust said.

"Can't win if you don't play," the Deputy said, watching Florence walk down the path. Then he snapped to attention as a bug flew by his ear. "Are there any bees around here? I'm allergic to bees."

***

Abdel looked at himself in the speckled mirror at dusk. He held the mask up and felt the surge of cold power run through his body.

As he touched the wood to his face, he saw blood dripping off of the trees like rain. Bodies were scattered across the campground. Horrified law enforcement took quivering steps through the macabre debris as the lake gently lapped against the shore.

He pulled the mask away and tucked it into his top drawer. Like a battery fully recharged, the voice roared through his mind.

Find the girl.

Abdel headed toward the main cabin where Florence was staying. He stopped by the utility shed and grabbed a saw, a level, a drill, and a handful of nails. Carrying the equipment, Abdel was almost in awe of how easy it was to find dangerous tools in plain sight.

Florence ushered Abdel inside. She had recently showered because the bottom of her hair was damp, and she smelled like chemical flowers.

"Thank you again for doing this," she said. "Are you hungry? I've got some food going."

The voice in his head began screaming.

Tell her the food smells delicious.

"I'd love some. Whatever that is."

"Lamb chops, rice pilaf, and homemade apple sauce."

Make a joke, the voice demanded.

"See? Some lambs do go to slaughter," Abdel said, and then smiled. Florence laughed harder than he was expecting, so much so that red wine leapt out of her glass and doused the keyboard of her laptop, which open. She was looking at bright yellow rain slicks.

"Whatever you think is the best way to go about this is fine for me," Florence said, leading him to the window that needed a shade. A faded floral comforter was perfectly made across the full-sized bed. A single lamp was glowing orange on top of a wooden nightstand. Abdel set the tools near the window.

"You already have rods up here," he said, pointing to the pre-existing track. "All we really need is curtains. No building or drilling necessary. "

"Okay, confession," Florence said, looking at the ground and swirling her wine glass. "I maybe wanted an excuse to get you here. I figured I could take down the curtains and then put in a work order with Joust. Because the window is tall, and Joust doesn't like carrying step ladders, he'd send you instead."

"Impressive planning," Abdel said. "It's like you had a voice guiding you."

Whoops, the voice said.

"Voice? What voice? Do you think I hear voices? I am NOT crazy!" Florence said, dropping her arms and heaving from the chest.

"I never said you were crazy," Abdel said, palms up.

"Just that I hear voices. The divorced woman hearing voices, probably why her marriage failed, right? Crazy chicks are great in bed, right? Well, how about you get out?"

Abdel stood up, flabbergasted.

"What do you want from me?"

"Just fix my campsite," Florence growled, then stormed into the living room where a pop from the fireplace sounded like a gunshot. Tucked into the back of her pants was a different wooden mask, and Abdel's eyes lit up.

"I have one, too!" he shouted as a real gunshot rang out, and Joust started screaming.

The Deputy hunched over Joust, who had been shot through the thick meat of his thigh.

"I thought he was a bear," the Deputy said, and radioed for an emergency med-evac.

Abdel looked at the blood squirting from the wound like a broken water fountain at a public park. It leaked onto freshly fallen green pine needles turning them orange.

Florence didn't talk to Abdel for three days, despite his attempts to make things right. Everything he did seemed to make it worse.

"Crazy history of this place," he said on the fourth day as Florence walked by holding two large trash bags full of insulation.

"Oh, and we should have sex?! If the world is ending, we might as well screw?! Well, virgins survive slasher films, Abdel, so keep dreaming," she said.

She hasn't seen Scream, the voice in Abdel's head said.

"Not what I was getting at," he whispered.

A few days later, Abdel spotted the Deputy walking with Florence near the recently rebuilt dock. She was barefoot, her jeans rolled up below her knees and soft ankles dipping in and out of the quiet shallows. The Deputy was throwing rocks as far as he could out into the water and pointing out how far he had thrown them. Florence smiled but looked into the hills.

That evening, when Florence was sitting at the picnic table eating alone, Abdel took a chance.

"If this were a slasher film, I'd be wary of the Deputy," he said.

"If we were characters in a slasher film, you wouldn't tell me who the killer was before the reveal."

She hasn't seen Scream, the voice in Abdel's head growled.

"I found a mask in the wall of one of the cabins, and it's been telling me what to do," he said.

"Oh real funny. A comedian. Did you overhear me talking with the unnamed Deputy about what I found?"

"Don't you think it's weird that he doesn't have a name? Doesn't matter. I found a mask, too. In bunk six, tucked inside of a wall panel."

"Leave me alone, Abdel. I liked you, okay? I liked your vibe, I liked your look, and...I don't know. Thank you for the work that you've done, but it's best if we keep forging our own paths that don't cross anymore."

She stood up. Florence didn't see Abdel's hurt or wild disbelief.

Prove to her your power... the voice said, and Abdel could feel the tickle of anger pushing against the front of his skull. If Florence didn't believe him, he would show her the truth, that he *did* have a mask, and he was hearing voices.

Inside of the bunkhouse, Abdel put the mask on and felt the temperature drop. The skies darkened as drops of rain clinked against the glass. Lightning crashed. The world outside shrank into a small tunnel.

Abdel hulked down the path. Life was too lonely to go at it alone, and if something bound him to his beautiful employer, then he needed to take that chance. In that moment, he almost understood why his wife left him for his old boss Billy. It didn't take away the pain, but it became clearer that life was about taking unexpected chances.

A lightning bolt had struck a nearby tree and caused it to fall over, smoking from the branches. Small pockets of flames danced around the notches, and the notches were pressed up against her front door.

Machete... the voice commanded, and Abdel took off in a full sprint toward the utility shed. He kicked down the door and pulled the machete from the leather satchel on the shelf. It sang a metallic hymn as he ran back out into the dark.

It was hard work running that fast, so he slowed down and opted instead to take giant steps forward at a quicker, more ominous pace. For safety, he kept the machete pointed at the ground, and when the terrain was tough, he let it drag behind him.

Once at the front door, he hacked at the downed tree sending shrapnel of bark in every direction. The branches cracked and the sideways tree rolled away. Abdel kicked open the door and stood in the frame with his mask on, wielding a machete, as lightning and rain tore open the sky.

Standing in the center of the room was Florence. She had her mask on, too. In her hand was an axe.

"You beat me to it," she said. Her voice was muffled by the wood.

"I wasn't lying to you," Abdel said.

Abigail... the voice in his head sang. *We're together at last.*

"Who is Harvey?" Florence asked, pushing the mask on top of her head.

I'm Harvey, Abdel's voice said.

"I think it's my mask. Yours must be Abigail?"

"The original suspects from the 1980's killing," Florence said, wide-eyed. "They didn't want us to maim and murder. They just wanted to be together again!"

"And in doing so, they brought us together," Abdel said, pushing his mask on top of his head.

"They're not cursed or haunted. They're just pining for love," Florence said.

"I mean, I think they're definitely haunted and cursed," but before he could finish, Florence had her palms on the side of his face, kissing him.

They kissed until they couldn't breathe so that it felt like they were drowning in the lake as counselors watched from their canoes.

"You know," Florence said, when she pulled away, "we should scare the shit out of the Deputy. I found out his name, by the way. It's Dewey."

"Like in *Scream*?" Abdel asked.

"I've never seen it." Florence shrugged.

Told you, the voice echoed.

"How have you seen *Scream*?" Abdel asked the mask. "You died in the 80's."

Internet, the voice replied.

Deputy Dewey was cautiously pacing in front of the lake. His gun was drawn.

"Hello?" he shouted. "My father was the original officer on scene during the 1980's massacre here, so I know more than you think I know!"

Two silhouettes emerged from behind a tree. One wielded a machete, one had an axe. They walked toward the shore.

"You think you have all of the answers," the masked man said.

"You think you can get away with watching hot, fully empowered and definitely not crazy divorcés change inside of their cabins?" the masked female asked.

"And also, what type of bear is only four feet tall and makes dumb puns all day?!" the man asked.

"Don't move!" The Deputy pointed his gun and radioed a code 133.

Florence noticed a swarm of bees buzzing on a branch above the Deputy's head.

"Actually, you don't move," she yelled and pointed. Dewey looked up and cursed.

"What do you want with me?" he asked.

"I think he's scared enough," Abdel said.

"Truce?" Florence called out.

"Never," the Deputy said and fired two shots.

The first bullet missed, but the second hit Abdel's large shoulder and sprayed hot blood into his face. On reflex, he cocked his arm and hurled the machete, cutting the beehive off of the branch. It landed with an explosion of furious bees that began to sting Dewey without mercy. He collapsed into the sand and rolled around flailing. Then, he was still.

"Is he...dead?" Florence asked.

"They're never dead," Abdel said. He lurched over to the scene and knelt down next to the body. In the distance, they both heard the sound of emergency vehicles. Florence jogged over and touched Abdel on the shoulder. It made him jump, which sprayed blood onto her face, too.

"Isn't this the part of the movie where the killer makes a pun? Where's Joust when we need him?" she said, shivering.

"Hive bee-n waiting," Abdel said, grinning.

Dewey survived. Abdel's shoulder was sewn up. The bullet had passed straight through. No charges were formally filed.

"What are y'all doing out there, anyways?" a nurse at the hospital asked. "Are you building a weekend long interactive storyline escape room or something? Because that sounds like a really awesome idea."

"It's more for yoga retreats and..." Florence started, but Abdel waved her off.

"What if we told you we were?" he asked.

"I'll tell you what, I'd pay good money to be part of a weekend long interactive storyline escape room on the site of an actual serial murder from the 80's."

"Sir, today is your lucky day because we are building a weekend long interactive storyline escape room."

The nurse lit up.

"I gotta go tell my kids," he said, pulling out a cell phone.

"It's a good thing you haven't built that website yet." Florence laughed and kissed the back of Abdel's hand.

In the hallway outside, Joust walked by pushing his IV. No one noticed because they had shaved off his beard and cut his hair, which made him look like an older version of Jamie Kennedy from *Scream*.

W. T. PATERSON

W. T. Paterson is a three-time Pushcart Prize nominee, holds an MFA in Fiction Writing from the University of New Hampshire, and is a graduate of Second City Chicago. His work has appeared in over 90 publications worldwide including The Saturday Evening Post, The Forge Literary Magazine, The Dalhousie Review, Brilliant Flash Fiction, and Fresh Ink. A semi-finalist in the Aura Estra short story contest, his work has also received notable accolades from Lycan Valley, North 2 South Press, and Lumberloft. He spends most nights yelling for his cat to "Get down from there!" Visit his website at www.wtpaterson.com.

Hoyt Family Vacation

Alexander C. Bailey

"**A**re you sure about this, Momma?" Lester asked for the hundredth time since they entered the sewers near their house.

"Of course, I'm sure, sonny. This family has been hard at work, and we deserve a vacation," Momma said from her perch on Lester's back. The family had designed the harness after Momma lost her legs chasing a teenage victim through their cornfield. The conniving bitch ran over Momma's legs with a thresher before Chucky had a chance to pull her from the cab. The family got their revenge though. Lester peeled the skin from the woman's legs and turned it into jerky.

"Lester, how many times have I told you not to question Momma? She's the smartest woman on the planet and knows what's best for us," Chucky said from behind Lester. He was carrying an oversized backpack full of supplies for the weekend along with the head of their pappy in a jar. "Who's the person that's kept us fed over the years?" Chucky asked.

"Momma," Lester replied. He scratched his sealed up left eye. He did this when he was nervous or whenever puss leaked out.

"Who convinced us that hunting would be good for us?" Chucky asked.

"Momma."

"Who convinced us that human beings are just another form of livestock we can live off of?"

"Momma."

"So, if Momma said this vacation was a good idea, don't you think she's right?" Chucky asked with anger in his tone. He was a complete momma's boy. He would and had done anything he could to protect his Momma. The day after her legs were cut off, he went into the barn where they kept the livestock chained up and beat on one until its face was a bloody pulp. He felt like he failed Momma and no one, not even her, could convince him otherwise. Ever since he'd been extra protective of the women who gave birth to him.

"Yeah, I guess," Lester said on the verge of tears. He hated when Chucky was mad at him. He sometimes wondered whether Chucky forgot that Lester's brain didn't work right or if he just didn't care.

"Ain't no guessing about it, little brother. Momma's always right," Chucky said.

"Now boys, quit your fighting. We don't want to start this trip off on the wrong foot. Apologize to each other before I whoop both of your butts red," Momma scolded from her harness.

"Sorry, brother," Lester mumbled. He didn't feel like he had anything to be sorry about, but he didn't want Momma to beat him again. His bottom was still sore from the last time.

"I'm sorry too, little brother," Chucky said.

Lester knew he didn't mean it but didn't say anything. Despite being years older than Chucky, the younger man called Lester his little brother whenever he was angry with the goliath.

The head in the jar watched the exchange with blinking eyes.

"We've walked for almost a day now. I think we're here. Chucky, put your bag down and take a peek out of this here manhole cover. Let's see if we're in the city or not," Momma ordered.

"Yes, Momma," the most normal of the family said before putting down his overstuffed pack.

While the rest of the family had obvious signs of mutation, Chucky's was easier to conceal. He was born with a second face stretched across his stomach. Momma guessed, having never taken him to a doctor, that Chucky was supposed to have a twin, but the twin was absorbed by Chucky. All the normal holes a face had were filled with skin on his stomach.

The youngest of the Hoyt family lifted the heavy metal manhole cover with ease. Thankfully, the family had decided to travel at night. Looking around, he saw buildings that were rundown and boarded up, but they were indeed in the city.

"We made it," Chucky said after replacing the cover and climbing back down to his family. "Want me to go ahead and find us a place to stay?"

"Nonsense. We're on vacation. We'll all go," Momma said in a joyful tone. She was the happiest she had been since Lester brought back his first kill with his Pappy. This was the first time she had been able to take her kids away from the farm ever. Her brother Jedidiah agreed to watch over the homestead and the surplus of human livestock that had been acquired over the last couple of weeks. Recently, a large group of hikers had stumbled upon the Hoyt family hunting ground. Living in the middle of nowhere Texas, they didn't have to worry about local law enforcement coming out to search their property for missing travelers.

Even if they did, Jedidiah knew what to do.

"Chucky, you climb up first and make sure the coast is clear," Momma tittered.

The younger man nodded and climbed back up the ladder and out the hole into the road.

"Momma, I don't know if I can fit up there," Lester said with a quiver in his voice.

"Sure, you can, my special boy. Remember that time the livestock got out and tried to escape through that drainpipe?" Momma cooed. "It was a tight fit, but you were able to grab onto his leg and pull him back. Momma was so proud of you."

Lester laughed softly at the memory and praise from his Momma.

"It's clear," Chucky called down to the rest of his family.

"Lester, be a good lad and hand your brother the bag. Be careful of your father now."

"Yes, Momma," Lester said before bending over to pick up the bag. He gently pushed the jar containing Pappy's head inside before pulling the drawstrings closed. He handed it up to Chucky's waiting arms. The two men had to push and pull the large bag through the hole, but eventually got it onto the road.

"Now, gently hand me up," Momma instructed.

Being even more careful than he had been with Pappy, Lester gently took Momma off his back and handed her up to Chucky. She fit through the hole without a problem.

"Okay, sweetie. Now it's your turn," Momma said down through the hole. "You got nothing to be scared of."

"Hurry up, you big galoot. We don't have all night," Chucky grumbled. He kept looking around expecting someone to see them. He was always wary of what the cattle would think when they saw his family. He was aware they would likely hunt them down and kill them.

"Don't rush him, Chucky." Momma swatted her youngest on the back of the head.

"Sorry Momma," Chucky said as he rubbed the spot where he was hit.

"I'm coming, Momma," Lester's voice echoed up from the hole. The pair at the top watched as the larger brother mounted the ladder and started climbing.

He got stuck about halfway through.

"What the fuck is that?" J.C. asked, stopping in place when he saw the largest man he had ever seen squeeze his way through a sewer hole and onto the street.

"What?" Oscar asked, looking up from his phone. He had been swiping on a dating app. His mouth fell open when he saw what J.C. was pointing at. Oscar closed the app and brought up his camera to take a video.

"Come on. Let's hide over there," J.C. said, nodding at some stairs leading to a boarded-up building.

Oscar kept his camera going. When they reached their hiding spot, he zoomed in to get a better look at each member of the group. He gasped when he saw the face of the large man. Not only was he missing an eye, but half of his face was also exposed down to the bone. Oscar had no idea how the man was not screaming in constant pain. The smaller man lifted his shirt, and Oscar was able to get the second face on camera.

"Holy shit, did you see that?" J.C. asked.

"Fuck yeah I did. I recorded it too."

The pair watched as the half-woman was placed on the large man's back. The smaller double-faced man looked around before placing a large pack on his back. The trio walked off into the night.

"Good. We need to show Don Mando," J.C. said before standing back in front of the steps. "I have a feeling this is going to be a long night."

"And why are you bringing this to me?" Don Armando, head of the Mando Mafia, asked after the video stopped.

"Well, Don Mando, I think I know who those people are," J.C. said. "Have you ever heard of the legend of the Hoyt family?"

Don Mando shook his head in the negative.

"Well, as legend has it, they are a family of cannibals that live somewhere in the middle of Texas. They are said to kidnap and eat people."

"Why should we care?" Armando asked, steepling his fingers.

"First, there is a reward for any information about the Hoyt family." Armando opened his mouth to speak, but J.C held up a hand to stop him. "I know we don't need the money, but it never hurts to be in good favor with the local law enforcement. Secondly, isn't it our responsibility to protect our customers in this city? There's no telling how much carnage the Hoyt family will cause in town. My guess is they're looking for a new hunting ground. We can't let that happen."

Oscar was sitting next to J.C. nodding the entire time. He knew to let J.C. do the talking.

The two men waited in silence for Armando to reply.

"Alright J.C., what do you suggest we do?" the Don finally asked.

J.C. let out a sigh before speaking. He knew this was coming and had been working out a plan since he saw the Hoyt family.

"Let's take no chances and go out in full force. Get everyone who owns a gun behind us. I want everyone. We track them down and fill them full of lead," J.C. explained. "My guess is the first thing they'll do is find a new place to stay. Either on purpose or by luck, they ended up in the perfect part of town. There's enough run-down buildings here. They could easily squat up in any of 'em."

"On that note, how will we be able to find them again?" Armando asked, leaning back in his chair.

J.C. shrugged. "It should be easy to find a seven-foot mutant freak carrying a woman with no legs on his back. All we have to do is canvas the area. When we find whatever building they're in, we surround it and kill them. Make sure to give them no chance of escape."

Armando took his time to think before he replied.

"Make it happen."

⸻

"Momma, this place is perfect." Chucky giggled. They had been walking most of the night before finding a place to stay while they were in town. It was a two-story house with peeling paint and overgrown weeds in the front yard. The fence surrounding the yard was rusted, and parts of it were falling apart. "We can stay here for as long as we want."

"That's why I picked it, son. Now let's go inside and make ourselves at home," Momma said with a smile.

Chucky led the way. He was the one Pappy had taught to pick locks and was able to unlock the front door with ease.

"Honey, I'm home," Chucky called out into the darkness.

The inside of the house was just as dilapidated as the outside. The living room was full of broken down and torn furniture left behind by the last occupants. Chucky let the backpack fall off his shoulders before he explored the rest of the house. The jar with Pappy's head rattled around, but he was thankful the glass didn't crack. He looked in the kitchen and was excited to find a stove and fridge. Without power, the appliances wouldn't work, but that didn't matter. The Hoyt family didn't need a lot of gadgets to be happy. Chucky turned on the faucet and was excited to see the water was still on. There was even enough counter space for him to efficiently prep meals. Most of the cabinets had doors hanging off them, and most of the insides were covered in rat droppings and spider webs.

There were three rooms on the second floor, two bedrooms and a dirty bathroom. Each bedroom had a twin-sized metal frame complete with a dirty mattress. The bathroom had a water-stained toilet and tub.

This is even better than what we have at home, Chucky thought.

To the outside world, this place was a rundown shithole. To the Hoyt family, it was better than the Ritz.

"I think I'm going to like it here," Momma said. "Now, we need to get something to eat. I don't know about you boys, but I'm famished."

It had been three days since the Hoyt family settled into their temporary home. Momma had claimed one of the beds while Chucky took the other one. Lester slept on the floor next to Momma's bed. He didn't care where he slept as long as he had his stuffed teddy bear. It was a ratty thing missing an eye and covered in blood, but he loved it.

They placed Pappy's jar on the only shelf left on the wall in the living room. Momma made sure that his face was pointed away from the wall.

The first night Chucky went out wearing an oversized trench coat and cowboy hat to conceal his face. In the front left pocket of the coat, he kept a bag and some rope. In the front right, he kept a large hunting knife. While he preferred to take his cattle alive, he wasn't afraid to get his hands bloody.

Taking on the role of the hunter, Chucky walked around the block the house was located on before expanding his search. He kept track of all the people living in the alleys and on the street. There was no telling how long Momma wanted them to stay, so he wanted to know where to easily get food.

His first victim was an older drunk who was singing loudly into the night. Chucky preferred younger meat, but the noise coming from this human-cow made him angry.

"Spare some change friends?" the drunk asked when Chucky stood next to him.

"Sure, buddy. I got a whole lot of cash back at my place. I even got a hot shower for you, too," Chucky replied, still keeping his face hidden.

"I usually don't swing that way, but how much cash are we talking about?" the bum asked, looking up at Chucky.

Chucky had to take a few moments to think about what would be considered a large amount of money. The only time he had to worry about the concept of cash was when he took it off the cattle. He thought about the largest amount he had found on well-dressed livestock.

"How about a thousand dollars?" Chucky asked.

"You got a deal, sonny," the bum said before standing up. "Lead the way."

Chucky led the bum back to the house. The homeless man talked the entire time. Chucky grunted when appropriate but overall said as few words as he could get away with. By the time the pair reached the house, Chucky's blood was boiling. He almost gutted the man in the front yard. What stopped him was knowing Momma would be angry. Instead, he led the man inside. When the bum's back was turned to the kitchen doorway, Lester popped out and hit him over the head with the small club he'd packed before they left their home.

Lester hit the man a few more times until the bum stopped twitching.

When the cow finally died, Momma and Chucky went to work preparing the meat.

This was how the Hoyt family spent four days of their vacation. Lester even convinced Momma to let him join Chucky on one of the hunts. Chucky argued that his giant brother would make the hunt more difficult but stopped when Momma told him Lester was going and that was final. Momma wanted Lester to see what he could do in the city.

It was due to the combination of people going missing, and a soldier of the Mando Mafia spotting Lester, that the group located the Hoyt family.

They spent the next day getting ready to take them down.

"Are you sure about this, boss?" J.C. asked as the limo headed toward the Hoyt hideout. They were sitting in the back of the vehicle; J.C. and Oscar were facing Don Armando. "I'd feel more comfortable if you'd stayed behind."

"Relax J.C. I'll be fine. I know it's been years since I did work on the streets, but I still know how to handle myself," the older mob boss said. "Besides, if we take these bodies to the cops, I want them to know who did their job for them."

J.C. just nodded. He knew better than to argue with his boss. Oscar was getting the guns ready as the two men talked. Both men normally carried Colt 1911 pistols. On top of that, they were going in with pump-action shotguns with the barrels sawed down. When both shotguns were loaded, he handed one to J.C. and kept the other in his lap.

Three more cars filled with four men each followed behind the limo. The plan was to circle the block and attack the house from each side. One man in each of the cars was armed with military-issued M4 assault rifles. They were going to empty their clips into the house. Once that was done, the rest of the men would move into the house and clear it out.

They knew they had the numbers to do this without a problem.

The limo parked in front of the house while the rest of the cars got into position.

"Alpha team ready," a female spoke through the radio piece in J.C.'s ear.

"Bravo team ready," another voice said.

"Charlie team in position, and I have eyes on the big one."

J.C. rolled down the widow halfway before speaking into his radio mic.

"All teams open fire."

Lester thought he saw someone standing outside the kitchen window before the glass and wall around the window exploded in a swarm of angry bees. The giant didn't know what to do until he heard Momma's voice over the multiple sounds of thunder.

"Lester, drop to the floor now!"

Without even trying to catch himself, the giant thudded to the ground. He felt what he recognized as bee stings on his way down.

He couldn't help himself and started to cry.

Chucky had been taking a bath in the stained tub when the assault started. He jumped from the tub and still naked, ran to the top of the stairs. He was able to see Momma drop the short distance to the floor as the walls around her exploded in what he knew were bullets. The attackers must have expected their targets to be on the first floor because no bullets had made their way through the walls upstairs.

Chucky ran back to his room and grabbed the two extra blood-stained knives he kept in his bag. The rest were in the kitchen.

The shooting stopped by the time he reached the stairs again.

"Lester, get in here!" Momma yelled from the living room.

The kitchen door was kicked open before the giant could pull himself up off the ground.

A man and woman holding guns entered the room. Before Lester could plead with them, they started shooting. The last thing that went through Lester's head, besides a bullet, was the thought that he wouldn't be able to hug Momma one more time.

Meanwhile, the front door crashed open, and two men entered. They started aiming at Momma until Chucky let out a war cry and charged them. They turned to aim at him, but the naked Hoyt family member was able to cross the distance before they got a shot out. He sliced each of their throats. Blood sprayed, dousing Chunky in the red liquid.

The pair from the kitchen had reloaded and made their way into the living room behind Chucky. They started to aim at the blood-covered man but turned when they heard Momma shriek from the top of the couch.

She caught a glimpse of Lester's body lying bleeding on the kitchen floor.

Chucky turned and snarled at the new intruders. He rushed forward using his body to slam into the two shooters. All three hit the ground. In a blind fury, Chucky stabbed his knives repeatedly into the bodies underneath him.

He didn't notice that two more men entered the house until the barrel of a gun was placed against his head.

There was a second where Chucky stopped stabbing, and he experienced an unknown feeling. Had he time to process it, he would have recognized it as fear.

Instead, his head was blown apart before he got that far.

The shrieking from Momma grew tenfold.

"Shut her up!" J.C. yelled to Oscar over the noise of the half-woman. Her screams were cut off by two blasts from Oscar's gun.

The surviving members of the Mando Mafia teams cleared the house before J.C. spoke into his radio mic to the driver of the limo. It was safe for Don Armando to come in.

J.C. was staring at the head in the jar when his boss walked in. The bodies of the Hoyt family had been pulled into the living room and laid next to each other. Armando looked them over before nodding and leaving the house to call his contact in law enforcement.

"Hey, I found something," Oscar said as he descended the stairs. J.C. saw he was holding a tattered notebook in his hands. In childish, misspelled handwriting, the cover read *Family Vacation*. J.C. flipped through the book to see drawings done in crayon along with scribbled words describing what the family had been doing since they came to town.

"Looks like they picked the wrong place to take a vacation." J.C. chuckled.

The soul of Pappy looked out of his jar with his dead eyes and wondered what was going to happen to him.

All he knew was he was still hungry.

ALEXANDER C. BAILEY

Alexander C. Bailey is a newer author, from Iowa. Currently, he has only short stories published, but is planning on publishing more in the coming days.

If you like to get to know Alexander follow him on Twitter @AlexFromIA

More books from 4 Horsemen Publications

Horror, Thriller, & Suspense

Alan Berkshire
Jungle

Hell's Road

Erika Lance
Jimmy

Illusions of Happiness

No Place for Happiness

I Hunt You

Maria DeVivo
Witch of the Black Circle

Witch of the Red Thorn

Witch of the Silver Locust

Mark Tarrant
The Mighty Hook

Steve Altier
The Ghost Hunter

Anthologies & Collections

4HP Anthologies
Teen Angst: Mix Vol. 1

Teen Angst: Mix Vol. 2

My Wedding Date

The Offices of Supernatural Being

The Sentient Space

Demonic Carnival

Demonic Classics

Demonic Vacations

Demonic Medicine

Demonic Workplace

& more to follow!

Demonic Anthologies
Demonic Wildlife

Demonic Household

XXX- Holiday Collection
Unwrap Me

Stuffing My Stocking

Discover more at 4HorsemenPublications.com